About the Author

H. Eugene is an author and poet from Detroit, MI. He hopes that through his writing, he can reach and affect many. What you will find in his books is a renewed and fresh perspective of storytelling.

Please visit his website for information on exciting new projects at mrnovels.com

Also by H. Eugene

The Trifecta: God Will Never Forget This Day

Here are some of the reviews of this truly original and thoroughly entertaining novel.

"The Trifecta is well-written. A unique plot with intriguing characters. The story is an ingenious thriller that will captivate you. Well done!"

"Well written and based the most significant historical story ever written."

"A thought provoking read which ends with a sense of hope for the future despite the world's imperfections."

"This is a book that will make you think."

SERI@L No Milk

H. Eugene

For information contact; mr.novels.com

ISBN: **0692563911**

ISBN-13: **978-0692563915**

H. Eugene

Dear Reader,

Thank you for taking another journey with me. I promise you that this trip will be thoroughly entertaining.

Seri@l No Milk introduces a new protagonist named Brooke Hannah. She is an investigative reporter with passion, pizazz, and most importantly integrity. This book marks the first of three adventures for our young journalist. What makes her even more special, is that she was named after my daughters, Brooke and Hannah.

Prepare to have your mind blown away. Prepare to have your mouth drop open. Prepare to be thrilled as you go on an unbelievable ride with Brooke Hannah. Wait until you see what's coming. And please by all means leave me a review if you've enjoyed what you read.

Dedication

This book and this series is dedicated to my twin daughters, Brooke and Hannah. I love you both always and forever. This character was created with many of the wonderful qualities that each of you display every day of my life. Thank you for helping me bring Brooke Hannah to life on paper.

"It is impossible to suffer without making someone pay for it; every complaint already contains revenge."

Friedrich Nietzsche

H. Eugene

The Daily Loser

Some lives simply aren't worth living

I Wish I Never Had You

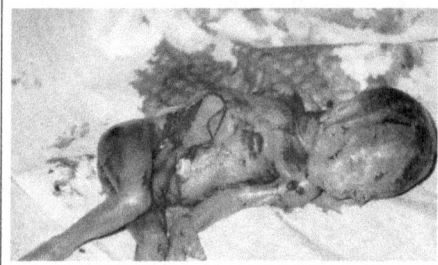

I Hate You

Losers like you don't deserve to breathe. Why do you continue to waste everyone's time? You are the worst mistake of my life.

```
6  x  3  =  9  6  x  3  =  9  6  x  3  =  9  6  x  3  =  9
6  x  3  =  9  6  x  3  =  9  6  x  3  =  9  6  x  3  =  9
6  x  3  =  9  6  x  3  =  9  6  x  3  =  9  6  x  3  =  9
6  x  3  =  9  6  x  3  =  9  6  x  3  =  9  6  x  3  =  9
6  x  3  =  9  6  x  3  =  9  6  x  3  =  9  6  x  3  =  9
6  x  3  =  9  6  x  3  =  9  6  x  3  =  9  6  x  3  =  9
6  x  3  =  9  6  x  3  =  9  6  x  3  =  9  6  x  3  =  9
6  x  3  =  9  6  x  3  =  9  6  x  3  =  9  6  x  3  =  9
```

You Repulse Me

Please don't make me say those names mama I hate those names … Ok, I'll say it! I'm a loser, I'm pathetic, I don't deserve to live, I'm ugly, no one likes me. I hate myself. I should kill myself …

Does That Burn?

No One Loves You

You're a Waste of Life

$6 x 3 = 9$ $6 x 3 = 9$ $6 x 3 = 9$ $6 x 3 = 9$
$6 x 3 = 9$ $6 x 3 = 9$ $6 x 3 = 9$ $6 x 3 = 9$
$6 x 3 = 9$ $6 x 3 = 9$ $6 x 3 = 9$ $6 x 3 = 9$
$6 x 3 = 9$ $6 x 3 = 9$ $6 x 3 = 9$ $6 x 3 = 9$
$6 x 3 = 9$ $6 x 3 = 9$ $6 x 3 = 9$ $6 x 3 = 9$

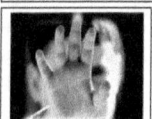

Mama I'm Sorry

I'm going to show you what happens to little clowns that don't listen. You will never forget what I did to you.

2

Prologue

Why is he making me do this? This is so sick... so sick. I just shaved off all that woman's beautiful hair with a shoddy pair of clippers. The blood is finally starting to dry. The other lady kept screaming and begging me to stop while I ripped out her eye lashes. Her eye is nearly swollen shut.

And that poor guy. Those blisters are sickening from that scolding hot water. He still can't move his arm. I can't take listening to the agony anymore. They're looking at me like I had a choice. I didn't want to do it. He was going to cut me open. What would they have done? Oh No! I hear his footsteps... he's back. What kind of maniac is this? What kind of game? Why me? Why us?

H. Eugene

Chapter 1

Mind over Matter

August 23, 2005 MSU Campus

The low humidity and just right temperature make this a perfect day for moving. Brooke and her family made the drive to East Lansing without incident. Arthur and Tina marveled at the relative ease of getting everything moved to her dorm room and unpacked.

They were both they met her roommate. Gwendolyn, and her parents. As Arthur looked around the quaint dorm, he knew that he was about to officially send his little girl off into a new world. He was extremely satisfied knowing she would be just fine.

But he wouldn't be a dad if he didn't have one last talk with his little girl. As the other parents and his wife laugh and converse, and Gwendolyn is busy unpacking her things, Arthur and Brooke take a walk of the campus outside.

"You know I'm really proud of you, right?"

Arthur gives Brooke a smile and raised eyebrow.

"Well, of course I do, dad. I hope now you realize that I was always listening to you and mom."

"I do realize that honey, and you've given me the perfect segue for what I wanted to talk about."

"Oh boy, here we go again, dad. Speech time."

"No, not really a speech, just something that's been on my mind for some time. I believe the time is right to share it. Ok, so it's a speech!"

They both laugh.

"Five years ago on your 13th birthday, your mom and I had the *Adult* conversation with you. Your mom shared her perspective from a woman's point of view, and I shared mine. I knew then, one day I would be having similar conversation with you, but with slightly different themes.

"Look, Brooke, you know that your mom and I have gone through some ups and downs financially. We are just now starting to recover. But even more than that, you've seen first-hand some of the sacrifices we've made over the years. These are sacrifices I hope you never have to make.

"There is this large part of me that prays your heart is never broken, you'll be surrounded by like-minded loving friends, and you'll build a solid career doing what you love to do.

"But then the realities of life start to kick in, and I realize that those experiences are all part of developing who you are and who you'll become.

"Brooke, nothing is for certain, and the game will change on you without regard or prejudice. Focus on doing all you can with your education. Then focus on building a career that's deeply rooted foundationally. The guys, the money, and the rewards will follow you. You will never have to chase after them.

"I want you to go and get'em with everything you have baby girl. Your mom and I love and believe in you. Have fun and enjoy the ride. Come here."

He gestured with his arms as he embraces his young lady.

Brooke always loved how her dad would speak volumes about something he could have gotten across in a few sentences. She heeded her dad's advice of making up front sacrifices to gain the greater good.

Her time spent at MSU helped to forge her passion for writing and journalism. All of the late-night studying paid off, as she remained at the top of her class. With some newly cemented connections, she worked a few days a week at the Ann Arbor Newspaper before they ceased publication.

On an early day May 8, 2009, Brooke Hannah received her Bachelor of Arts Degree in Journalism. This was a truly proud moment for her and her parents. Many of her friends and relatives turned out in droves to help her celebrate this special event.

Well before her graduation, Brooke had her eyes set on another educational target, one she knew wouldn't be a popular subject with her parents. She applied to and was accepted at the University of Florida for the journalism grad program.

It was a tough decision to leave home and everything she was familiar with. However, she knew to truly spread her wings, the move to Florida was the best one. True to form, although apprehensive, her parents were supportive and loving as usual. They both knew that leaving Michigan for Florida would spur the continued mature growth of their daughter. Besides, it gave them both a great place to visit.

Brooke was quickly courted for an internship at the Bay 9 News Channel, where she worked hard to make a name for herself. She was officially hired the day after receiving her Master's Degree.

H. Eugene

Chapter 2

I love Your Parents

May 16, 2010 Trade Winds Island Grand Resort

Iwant to thank you all once again for attending such an important event. And congratulations to this year's winners. For those that are interested, each member of our illustrious panel of speakers will be available for a question-and-answer session in the adjoining rooms just outside this door."

As the mayor bids a goodnight to the record crowd, there are many that move on to the speaker sessions. One of the speakers is Brooke, who was handpicked by the dean to attend on behalf of the school. Despite the jitters, she does an exceptional job with her speech, and in the subsequent Q&A forum.

There is one person that has waited patiently for Brooke to finish, choosing not to participate with the rest of the group.

"Good evening, Miss Hannah how are you doing? I wanted to wait for you to finish. I just had some questions I needed to personally ask you, if you can spare a few moments."

"Why sure." said Brooke as she extends her hand. "It's nice to meet you. What's your name?"

"Please don't be offended, but I don't shake hands with anyone. My hands are overly sensitive, and well. Can I ask you about your parents?"

"Umm, sure. What would you like to know?"

"You said they were your foundation. Can you describe what your parents were like?"

"Well, that's an easy question. They are super supportive and have always been interested in what's best for me. They have never tried to steer me in any direction I wasn't comfortable with; rather, they gave me the black and white choices and always explained how I may or may not benefit, based on what I chose.

"They also allowed me to make mistakes and not feel bad about them. They have always believed in me and there was never a second that I didn't know how much they loved me. That is what gives me strength when I need it most."

"So, you were always able to talk to both of them. They never made you feel insecure? They never embarrassed you?"

"Heavens no. Quite the opposite. I can honestly say I came from a very loving household."

Brooke can sense tension in the man's face and tries to redirect.

"Well, what about your parents? How were they the rocks of your foundation?

"I don't have fond memories like you do, Miss Hannah. My parents are both dead. They died when I was quite young. You are very lucky to have such a loving relationship. Some people would kill to be where you are. From the stories you told in your speech, to what you've just stated, I can tell that you love them very much. I suppose I do too. I love them for what I never had. Goodnight, Miss Hannah. It was a pleasure to meet you."

He quickly walks away.

"Hey Brooke, he seemed a bit odd." said Mitch, one of her counterparts. "What was his deal?"

"I feel a bit sorry for him. He lost his parents when he was quite young. Who knows what kind of life he's lived without them. You can tell that he misses the closeness of family. Maybe my story gave him hope."

"Yeah, if you say so. He seems a bit unhinged if you ask me. Come on, I will walk you to your car."

Chapter 3

The Pleading

December 2, 2012

Oh my God my head hurts. Travis? Lewis? Gordo? Where are you guys? Wait a minute my hands. What's wrong with my...... my hands!? What's going on? Somebody, help me. Where Am I?"

As the girl looks down at herself, she realizes her entire body is restrained in a chair. The lighting is dim, yet she can tell she is in a warehouse based on the extra tall ceilings. The room has a pungent and unfamiliar smell. Her attention turns quickly to the suddenly opened door.

"Keep that noise down or I swear I'm going to knock your damn teeth out. Shut up!"

"Where am I? Who are you? Please mister, where are my friends? What is this thing you have me in? Why are you doing this?"

The man quickly walks in front of the girl. She is meticulously restrained to a metal chair. Her head is able to move freely, as she looks at the man's face in terror.

"You see what this is you piece of trash? If you speak one more time without being spoken to, I'm going to sew your lips shut and I promise you it will hurt.

"I'm working on a little project right now and I need to finish with some finite details. Your little screaming tantrums have messed up my train of thought.

"You wanna know why you're here? It's because you and your friends are garbage. You are the lowest forms of filth because you prey on the innocent. You spit in the face of those that you pretend to care about. You're just like your stupid aunt.

"You think you're better than everyone else. You think just because you have money, you have the right and privilege to treat people anyway you see fit. We are nothing but gum on the bottom of your expensive shoes.

"All my life I've been the underdog. I was never good enough. Look at me! Do I appeal to you --- to your sexual urges? I think not, and I would rather be tortured than to have your filthy hands touch me anyway.

"There is no more getting away with it. There is no more mistake making. There are no more lies. I am sick of these lies." The man paces back and forth quickly while holding his hands over his ears.

"Is this fate? I wonder if this is not the most perfect example of it. I was definitely at the right place at the right time. You put on quite a performance earlier tonight. Do you remember that man you had your little altercation with? Tell me, is your bladder full again?"

The girl cries while being careful not to let the whimpers grow chorus.

"Do you want to say something Miss Piece of Trash?"

"Please mister. I'm so sorry that all happened. We had been drinking and we made some very poor choices. Please let us go. I promise you I will go and find that guy and apologize to him. I always keep my word."

"You really are just like your aunt. The same lies with the same straight and sincere face. And those tears do nothing for me. You want to make it right? You really want to make it right? Well guess what? It's too late. That poor man is already dead. He died because of you and your stupid friends. I had a chance to watch him take his last breath. Those are the people that you turn your backs on.

"Hey wait a minute… I know. You can and you will make it right. You and your friends can make amends for what you have done. Let's call a spade a spade.

"You won't need your arms or hands to enjoy this fun ride. All you need to do is relax. I'll even play a little music before we get started so you can knock off some of those jitters.

"Just sit back and relax. I will only require the removal of your head!"

Chapter 4

Tired of this Game

December 12, 2012

At some point in our lives we run into questions that remain unresolved," said the man, as he sits down in a recliner. "I believe I share the same tasks as all eight of you. We are trying to figure out if there is proper justification for our purpose.

"I've been speaking with each of you explicitly as we try to come to terms with the reality of poor planning and poor decision making. I spent most of my life in the shadows of make believe. And please don't look around in confusion with the things that you are surrounded with. They are superficial and diversionary. Money can buy you tangible things, but everything you see lacks substance.

"I long for simplicity, so I surround myself with over indulgent vestiges that serve nothing more than to give me a reminder of what I despise the most, Humanity.

"I have watched sheer savagery replace the human spirit. I don't know how or why we lost it, but we have been without it for a very long time. I must admit I sat on the sidelines and watched much of this animalistic behavior even as a young child. I tried to trick my eyes into thinking it wasn't real. But it was all too real, and I was a spectator.

"But no more. One day I decided to take a stance. That was the day we truly became one. All of you have gone far beyond

15

the point of return. These decisions that must be made, have already been made for you. You no longer need to worry about miscalculating your premise.

"As I look around at each of you, I realize people, the uninitiated, shall we call them, will say you have been victim to truly disgraceful or unfathomable deaths. And they will be wrong. Each of you were looking for sanctuary. You were looking for a means to bring color to this otherwise bleak black and white life of yours.

"Again, I have sat on the sidelines and have pondered with very little action. That ends today. I now have a solution for that which has puzzled me. And with that, I say thank you for providing me with the inspiration to do that which must be done.

"I'm ready to go home. I wonder where that is? Perhaps I will see you all again soon."

The man walks upstairs with a look of relief and peace. He takes out his cell phone and goes to the front porch to place a call.

"911 what's your emergency?" asked the operator.

"I like to report a murder. In fact, I'd like to report eight of them. I really took my time with them, so everything should be nice and neat. I'll be sitting on my front porch when the policemen arrive."

Chapter 5

The Sun-kissed Reporter

April 22, 2015 9:30am Office of the Editor

As Brooke walks through the main aisle of the Bay 9 news department, hundreds of fingers dance across the keyboards, as numerous voices are overheard jockeying for position for the best leads.

As she walks through, there are nods of admiration, as she is *the hot* reporter. She has built a firm and highly credible reputation during her 3 years of interning and nearly 3 years as one of their top investigative reporters. She is tall and flowing, with an uncanny resemblance to the late Dorothy Dandridge. Brooke is well respected for her intellect as well as her natural beauty.

Be that as it may, she is a bit nervous to meet the station manager for a rarely scheduled meeting. She is oblivious to its content.

"Good morning, Brooke, come right in and make yourself comfortable." said the station manager, Hank Bergdoll. "I'm sorry I had to move this meeting around a couple of times, but that Kramer story has everyone in disarray."

"No problem at all, sir."

"So, before we begin, the first thing I'm going to ask is that you relax your shoulders and sit back."

17

Mr. Bergdoll smiles hoping to calm Brooke, as it's obvious she has the jitters.

"Is it that obvious?"

She sits back in the chair doing her best to follow his advice.

"The good thing about news people is that we are always busy looking forward to the next *thing*. With that said, I will get right to the point. Brooke, since you started as an intern and we took the risk to place you out in the field as one of our investigative reporters, your work has been truly phenomenal. And now look at you, six years later.

"Now, of course, you are no stranger to these words, as you and I have had several conversations about your performance. You know that I'm going to have an open anchor position with the evening news, since Todd announced his retirement last week. Well, I want to offer it to you. What do you think?"

Brooke is completely blown away by the question she always dreamed of hearing. An anchor on the Bay 9 news channel is a once in a lifetime gig for any aspiring news head. A substantial increase in pay and a huge boost to her personal brand makes this a no-brainer. But something else is keeping her from giving the obvious commitment.

"Mr. Bergdoll, I don't know what quite to say. I am profoundly grateful for this opportunity. Since I was in high school, I always thought about what it would be like to be a news anchor. Clara Fox was by far my news idol back then. She exhibited the perfect balance of effervescence and effectiveness. I told myself that one day I would have the same chance. And now, today, you offer it to me."

"Brooke, why do I get the feeling that you're alluding to something different?" he asked, as he tries to understand her direction.

"My apologies, sir. I inherited the skill of storytelling from my father. I got it honest. Since I officially began my investigative work with this station just over three years ago, I have covered just about every kind of story you can think of. My first story was about a Bar Mitzvah. My favorite story was about a paraplegic receiving his degree. And my most trying story was the hostage standoff at Radcliff Bank and Trust.

"What I've come to realize is that I feel so alive out there in the field amongst the people. Amongst the everyday reality for so many. Sir, I know in my heart it's where I belong.

"This opportunity does not come around very often, and I realize this. But if you will allow me sir, I promise to give you the very best coverage out there beyond these walls. I will be the ideal partner out there for your anchor team. So, I guess I've said all of this to state, I respectfully decline your generous offer."

Mr. Bergdoll smiles and looks at Brooke with the utmost respect and admiration.

"I gotta tell you Brooke, in a way I'm not surprised that you are turning down this position. I believe you have found your rhythm and your calling. It takes a person of immense integrity to place the people's needs ahead of their own. Your opportunity will never go away. It will be there for you should you decide you want it.

"Well, since you turned me down you owe me one." he said with a smile. "You remember that serial maniac, Gainsborough?"

"Why, yes sir, I do. Who could forget that guy? He was a real piece of work."

"He's being executed this Friday and he requested an audience with a reporter. When I said you owed me one, I was just pulling your leg. You see, even if you accepted the anchor position, I was going to ask you for one last task. I need you to interview this guy and see what the heck he has to say. I know you are starting your vacation tomorrow, but I really need you for this one. The station will gladly reimburse you for any inconvenience this may cause."

"Sure Mr. Bergdoll, it is no inconvenience at all. I was getting the house in order and finishing a quick project before I left anyway. This won't interfere with anything. I must admit Gainsborough kinda gives me the creeps, but I'm all over this interview. I'm curious though, sir, why me?"

"Well, that's the strange part, Brooke. He requested you."

"What!? Really?" Brooke gasped. "How or why is he requesting me?

"That's what I need you to find out. Governor Mitchum called me personally late yesterday afternoon. I believe she has a vested interest in this since her niece was one of Gainsborough's victims. She pulled the necessary strings to get you access to him.

Chapter 6

Behind Closed Doors

Florida State Prison

As Brooke drives to the state prison, she can't shake the eeriness she feels from the conversation with her station manager, Mr. Bergdoll.

Why would a serial killer make a personal request to speak with me?

Although she is slightly overwhelmed with the request, she realizes that these are the types of stories that have firmly shaped her during her tenure with Bay 9.

"Hello, my name is Brooke Hannah with Bay 9 News, and this is my cameraman, Charlie. We are here to speak with Thaddeus Gainsborough."

"I know exactly who you are, Miss Hannah." remarked the guard. "We've been waiting for you. Everything is set up just beyond this hallway. The guards inside will give you a briefing."

A second guard walks Brooke and Charlie down the hall to a door on the right. As they enter, they are met with two guards standing at the entrance.

"You must be Miss Hannah. My name is Officer Thomas. I hate to tell you this, but you can't take any footage with that camera. You may use an audio recording device or old-fashioned pen and paper."

"No problem," said Brooke. "Charlie, let's just use the mic and audio for this one."

"You got it." said Charlie as he readies the audio device.

"There are some other ground rules that must be obeyed for everyone's safety." said the officer. "First of all, this interview is highly unusual, as we never do anything like this. This request is something straight out of the movies, but that's not my call. Mr. Gainsborough is just on the other side of that door. His hands and feet are bound to the chair, and he is flanked by four guards.

"You must maintain ten feet of distance at all times. There will be no physical contact of any kind. At any time, if you feel uncomfortable and want to end the interview, come right back through this door. Once you leave, the interview is over. I think that about sums it up. Do you have any questions before we begin?"

"No questions, we are ready to proceed." said Brooke.

As Brooke enters the door, she makes direct eye contact with one of the most vicious serial killers in modern times, and certainly in the state's history.

Thaddeus Gainsborough a successful local attorney snapped and murdered eight victims in a two-year period, which canvassed various parts of Florida. With each of his victims, they were beheaded, and their heads stuffed and shaped to make human bowling balls. He then took ten bowling pins and wrapped them in his victim's flesh. He displayed the severed remains in a makeshift bowling alley in the basement of the house.

There were no leads in the case, as the state was on high alert. In a tremendous turn of events, that to this day no one understands, he called the authorities to his home where he turned himself in without incident.

Thaddeus is 5'10 and portly. At first glance he looks like a nerdy science teacher. His hairline has receded to almost non-existence. He has no facial hair and is squinting with regularity, but not from the need of glasses. This appears to be more of a physical condition.

It's difficult to believe that someone so friendly looking and unassuming could be so cold and calculating.

He smiles at Brooke as if she is a long-lost friend. She takes a seat on the opposite end of a long metal table.

"Brooke Hannah. I am super impressed and just tickled that you dropped by for a visit." said Thaddeus. "You are a very pretty lady. Much more so in person."

"Um, thank you."

Brooke is a bit unnerved by the compliment.

"Oh, don't worry Brooke, I'm not some kind of psychotic that's trying to get into your head. There will be no mind games today. I simply want to converse with you. If you don't object, how about I start?"

"Please do so, Mr. Gainsborough. I hope you don't mind us recording the audio."

"Not at all. My only requirement for the duration of this interview is that you call me by my first name. There's no need for us to be so stuffy."

Chapter 7

The Inner Voice

Thaddeus slouches backward in the metal chair and smiles. He displays an unusual pleasantness for someone who will be executed in a few short hours. He will be the quickest prisoner to be put to death after trial in state history, merely 18 months after his sentencing. He attempted to move the proceedings up even faster, foregoing all of his legal rights; however, the judge would not grant his request.

"It's really not so bad in here. Everyone has been really nice to me. I don't have any friends because they have me isolated from the rest of the population. It makes me feel like I have the plague or something.

"But I get to read a lot, which more than makes up for the lack of friendship. I just finished reading my 300th book. There's not much else that interests me to read. They really need to expand on their selection here, it's a bit sparse. I suppose it's a good thing that today is my last day." Thaddeus quickly changes gears. "Would you mind if I played the reporter for a moment? I always wanted to be a reporter, but Bartholomew wouldn't let me."

"Sure Thaddeus." replied Brooke. "Let's see what you got."

"Ok, very good. My first question is why did I want to speak with you?"

"I'm sorry Thaddeus, I should have asked you for the rules of engagement before we switched. Am I supposed to answer your questions directly?"

"No, Brooke, you need to just sit and record for now. I'm talking to Bartholomew. He won't let me call him Bart for short. He insists on hearing his whole name. I think it's his narcissistic persona. He's going to give me the answers, and then I'm going to relay them to you. This is going to be so much fun!"

Brooke listens with interest, though she is quite confused as to whom Thaddeus is referring to when he mentions Bartholomew. Surely this is someone he's made up in his mind. The court appointed doctor declared him legally sane. This is surely perplexing.

"Brooke, you were invited here because Bartholomew admires you, though he won't tell me why. He would like you to hear his side of the story. He's not some depraved serial killer. He is a *Humanistic Engineer*. He specializes in human problem solving. The eight that were picked simply could not find resolution anywhere else. Bartholomew acquiesced and saved them.

"Eight down and now just five more to go, then Bartholomew can finally rest. There are so many problems, Brooke. It is a truly overwhelming venture. But these thirteen individuals reached out to him. There was no way he could turn them down. He's really compassionate in that way."

Brooke looks on with confusion as she tries to understand what he is referencing when he mentions thirteen.

"Bartholomew thinks that you might be the only person qualified to truly understand his humanistic approach. For some reason he favors you over me. That really makes me sad. I think it's because you're pretty and you smell good, but what do I know.

"OK, and for my last question… how can you help? Well, he says it all comes down to attention to detail. What are you willing to sacrifice, Brooke? How far will you go? And I believe that's all the questions I have for now. It's your turn now Brooke. Ask away. What's your first question?"

This interview is more awkward than she imagined. Prior to her arrival, she was a bit unnerved about meeting with a psychopath. But now, she almost feels pity for Thaddeus. She believes that he is truly insane and can't understand how the doctors couldn't see this. She wants to forge ahead so this interview can end. But first, she had to take her turn.

"Ok, Thaddeus, thank you. Can you tell me who Bartholomew is?"

"Hmm, I thought I already told you that. You must do a better job at listening. He is a Humanistic Engineer. He uses philosophy, theory and physics to problem solve."

"And where is he now, Thaddeus?"

"That's an easy question. He's hiding in the weeds like a little mouse. Say, have you ever read *Of Mice and Men*? Lennie coulda did that!"

Brooke manages a smile.

"I have read that book, Thaddeus. I remember it and Lennie quite well. So, Bartholomew is hiding. Is he afraid of something? Does he think someone is going to hurt him?"

There is a long pause before he answers.

"Please don't be offended by his statement, but Bartholomew doesn't believe you possess the intelligence to enter into mind games with us. Please don't placate us. Now, what's your next question?

"My apologies, I will continue. You mentioned there are a total of thirteen. Are you speaking about thirteen victims? There were only eight found at the house. Who are the other five, and are they alive?"

"They were never in any danger. They are the one's looking for help. Bartholomew is the only one that can give it to them. You know, sometimes Bartholomew is completely silent, yet I understand everything he's saying. Thirteen was always the plan. It's so nice when everyone comes together and cooperates."

"If it's help they wanted, Thaddeus, why did Bartholomew kill them? Why were their deaths the only way?"

"That's the point I'm trying to make, Brooke. They were not harmed in any way. They were released from this intrepid problem filled world. They came to Bartholomew for salvation. For the famous reporter that you are, your questions seem to be lacking, Brooke."

"I'm still unclear on what my purpose is in interviewing you. What is it that you want from me, Thaddeus?"

"I suppose this is a little boring, huh? The only thing that will be required of you is to do some reading. That will be the only way to prevent the other five from having their problems solved. The guards were so kind as to bring my copy down here. I want you to have it. I have read it many times. *Of Mice and Men* will provide you with some much-needed clarity.

27

"I will be long gone by the time you've finished reading it. Why don't you kick back and read it tonight, Brooke? Not everything is what it seems. It was a pleasure to meet you. You are a very nice lady. I believe outside of here you and I would have been friends, but we couldn't let Bartholomew know. He gets awful jealous sometimes.

"You know, I just thought about something. Bartholomew and I had two sets of our favorite toys. Our favorite by far was the Captain America action figure. If you were our friend that would mean all three of us would have had the same toy. Can you imagine how much fun we would have with three Captain America's? Well, I suppose it's time for me to take my last stroll. Good luck, Brooke. Oh wait! One last thing, I almost forgot. Bartholomew and I wanted to also say thank you for taking time to visit us while you're on vacation. Not many people would do that. This meant a lot."

Thaddeus motions to the guards that he'd like to leave, as they remove the restraints from the chair and escort him back to his cell. One thing Brooke has mastered over the years is how to remain perfectly stoic and calm. On the inside, she is completely frazzled on how Thaddeus knew she was on vacation. She peers over at the tattered copy of the classic work and places it in her purse. This interview is nothing like she expected.

He has a split personality. I suppose it's a good thing both will be gone very soon. And no, Thaddeus, I'm thinking we wouldn't be friends outside of here."

Chapter 8

Debrief

The Florida Governor's Mansion

It's a two-hour drive from the state prison to Governor Mitchum's mansion. This gives Brooke plenty of time to clear her head and try to make sense of what's happening. The governor asked if there could be an immediate debrief after the interview with Thaddeus.

There is nothing routine about any of this. She wondered why the governor was directly involved, though having her niece brutally murdered is certainly incentive enough.

Thaddeus was indeed a strange bird, she thought. He seemed just as pleasant and normal as anyone else. She wondered what the trigger was that would cause him to do such unspeakable things.

Still, there was something odd about him that she couldn't quite lay her finger on, and it had nothing to do with the voice named Bartholomew inside his head.

As she arrives at the mansion, she sees her station manager's car, and an unmarked police vehicle. She is escorted to the Florida Room of the mansion to give her debrief. Governor Mitchum, Mr. Bergdoll, and Police Chief Jared from St. Petersburg PD all rise to greet her.

"Brooke, thank you so much for everything you've done today." said the governor.

"It's my pleasure to be here governor. And hello to you Chief Jared. It's good to see you again."

"And Likewise, Brooke."

"Brooke, please have a seat and make yourself comfortable." said the governor. "Can I get you anything?"

"No governor, I'm fine but thank you for asking."

"Brooke, this has been a very trying time for my family as you can imagine. We will be able to conclude the ugly part of this chapter in a few short hours. The agony of my niece's death tortures me daily. The death of Gainsborough does nothing to ease my mind of this.

"But my apologies for allowing my emotions to get the best of me. You were invited here because the chief and I are quite curious about your conversation with Gainsborough. At the beginning of this week, I received a call from Gainsborough's court appointed attorney. He had a personal letter from Gainsborough that he wanted to deliver to me.

"Not only did this raise my ire, but more especially my curiosity. I thought naturally he had a change of heart and suddenly wanted to request a stay of execution. But no, that's not what the letter was about."

"Brooke, take a look at this letter." said Chief Jared.

He passes her a manila file folder with no markings. Brooke reads the letter to herself.

Hello Governor Mitchum,

I hope this correspondence finds you in both good health and spirits. I wanted to say how sorry I am for your loss. Your niece Valerie was a very sweet girl. Did you know that she never had one single cavity? That's quite an accomplishment for a 17-year-old.

Her death was the only one I had regrets about. You see, that automated blade mechanism that you undoubtedly heard about or may have even seen first-hand, got stuck half-way into her neck. I had to pry that thing out. Boy did she squirm. I decided to take my bat and cave her head in because it took less time. She is the only one that suffered. Everyone else went smoothly and efficiently.

In the end, I realized there was no end. The realities don't match the circumstances. I have a dream governor, but it's nothing like Dr. King's. Before I leave this place, there is something I need to share. I want a reporter on the day of my execution. I want to see them face to face. Send me Brooke Hannah. She is the only one that can stop the bleeding.

"Dear God governor. I'm so sorry. This letter doesn't sound like it came from the same person I interviewed."

"What do you mean?" Asked the chief. "How was he different?"

"It's really strange chief. The person I interviewed was very demure and gentle. He was friendly and non-confrontational. He kept talking to this person he created in his mind. Maybe this alternate personality is what's represented in this letter. How is it that he passed the psych exam? He effortlessly shifted between two different personalities right before my eyes."

"I realize this is an oxymoron," said the chief. "But a good psychopath can ace one of those exams. There are a number of tests that can be administered to make the determination. He passed all of them with flying colors. We are really interested to hear what he had to say to you, Brooke. Since his arrest, he hasn't shared anything until the governor received this letter. Did he tell you why he personally asked for you?"

"It was really cryptic what he said. He said his inner voice, whom he named Bartholomew, thought I was the only person who would understand his *humanistic approach*. He said he was a Humanistic Engineer that specialized in what he called human problem-solving."

"Did he mention anything about the killings or motive?" asked the chief.

"The only thing he mentioned was that those eight that were killed sought him out for help with their problems. He was very delusional."

"None of this makes any sense," said the governor. "Something is not adding up. I don't understand what type of game he is attempting to play. It will be over soon though. No more game playing."

"Brooke, what questions did you ask him?" asked Mr. Bergdoll.

"There was nothing standard about this interview, sir. He wanted to play by his own rules, though I must admit I was confused on what role I played in any of it. He left me with a copy of a book, *Of Mice and Men,* and recommended I give it another read. There was zero value in this interview I'm afraid. I believe my visit was purely for his entertainment. Probably the most interesting thing he said was thanking me for coming to interview him while I was on vacation. Did someone mention that to him?"

"Well, no Brooke." said Mr. Bergdoll. "I only mentioned it to the governor."

"Nor did I Brooke." replied the governor. "The only thing I mentioned to his attorney was that I couldn't guarantee you would be available."

"No worries. Perhaps I released something unknowingly. It was a rather bizarre interview. I'm sorry I came back empty-handed."

"Not at all Brooke." said the chief. You did us a great service today. You've helped cement how psychotic Thaddeus Gainsborough was. This nightmare will finally enter the healing phase very soon."

After the four met, Brooke drives back to her home to officially start her weeklong vacation. The next day before she leaves for the airport, she looks at the book, *Of Mice and Men*, but decides to leave it behind. There was simply no way she was going to read this book while relaxing to her first real vacation in nearly two years. Besides, she had already read the story three different times.

Lennie is still Lennie.

Chapter 9

Teatime

May 4, 2015 8:34pm

The trip back home was all Brooke needed to mentally recharge. Her parents have always refused to change her room. It's just as she left it, even the same two teddy bears on the white stool in the corner. It was tough on them when Brooke decided to move to Florida to continue her education. And when she took the job at Bay 9, her parents were extremely proud and devastated at the same time.

They missed their only child raising mayhem around the house. Having her back home for a nearly a week was blissful for them. Brooke's dad was especially living in the moment. This also gave Brooke an opportunity to catch up with many old friends and some of her favorite eateries. As much as she loves her new home in Florida, there is still something that makes her heart beat gentler here in the city of Detroit.

After a great time with her parents, Brooke flies back to Florida to enjoy her last evening of vacation before returning to work the next day. After dinner, she decides to get an early start on her backlog of emails. The doorbell rings.

"Just a minute." blurted Brooke, as she peers through the lookout on the front door. "Mr. Gregory!?"

She opens the front door to greet her next-door neighbor, Mr. Richard Gregory. Since his diagnosis with Alzheimer's last summer, he sometimes forgets where he is, becoming quite disoriented at times. This is the second time in the past three weeks that Mr. Gregory has walked out of his house and next door to hers.

"Hello, Mr. Gregory, how are you?"

"Hello Brooke, I was just about to make some tea, but I'm confused. Where is the teapot? And I think we might be out of tea bags too."

"Hmm. I think I can help you find that tea pot of yours and some fresh tea bags, Mr. Gregory. Give me one second while I grab my key, and then we'll take a walk and see what we can find."

"Oh dear, I really appreciate this, Brooke. I think Linda is trying to hide things from me."

"Now, now, Mr. Gregory. You know that your wife would never do such a thing. Ok, let's go find that teapot."

Brooke walks Mr. Gregory back next door. She finds he left the backdoor wide open. Mrs. Gregory is upstairs on the phone with her sister, and totally unaware that he had even left the house. Brooke finds everything she needs to make Mr. Gregory a nice pot of tea.

Afterwards, she returns home and continues to work on her backlog of emails.

Chapter 10

Neighborly Visit

The Next Night

The night couldn't be more perfect. The temperature is 66 degrees outside with a gentle breeze that feels free of humidity. The curtains blow and flirt effortlessly as Brooke enjoys the uncomplicated night. Her first day back at work was busy, yet uneventful. As she kicks back on the sofa to read, she receives a phone call from someone unknown.

"Hello, this is Brooke!"

"Hello Brooke, I'm afraid I'm lost and need some help." said a man with a very calm and articulate voice.

"I beg your pardon. Ok, who is this? How did you get this number? How do you know my name?"

"I need some help. I seem to have misplaced something."

The man speaks in the exact same pitch and inflection. He is plain and indistinct. Brooke sits up, as this caller now has her full attention. Something tells her this is not a prank call.

"Listen sir, I don't know how you got this number, but you're calling the wrong person. I'm afraid I can't help you.

"I am calling Brooke Hannah. For the last time, I lost something, and I need your damn help!"

The man's voice is abrasive and demeaning.

"Then why the hell are you calling me?"

She amazingly maintains her composure, though the aggravation is somewhat apparent in her response. The man's voice reverts back to calming decibels.

"I'm calling because I lost my teapot. Maybe your neighbor can help me find it. He's waiting for you on the front porch. You better check it out. Six times three equals nine." The call ends.

"Mr. Gregory!? No this is not happening."

She stares at the front door.

"This is not real. This can't be real. I'm going to call next door. This is a sick prank."

Brooke calls next door as she impatiently waits for someone to pick up the phone, but there's no answer.

"Come on." she begged. "It's no use, I'm going to have to walk over there."

As brave as she wants to be, she dreads leaving out of her front door. She takes the small bottle of pepper spray from her purse and nervously opens the front door.

"Phew, nothing there. There's no one here. Ok, on my way...... Oh God! Mr. Gregory!? You scared me.

To her right on the front porch swing sits Mr. Gregory. He has an empty teapot sitting on his lap. He is motionless with his head slouched to the side.

"Mr. Gregory, are you ok? Please say something. Are you sleeping?"

Brooke walks over to him and touches his face. He is cold and unresponsive. She jumps back!

"Oh no. This is not happening. This is not happening."

She takes out her phone and dials 911. Mr. Gregory is dead. *That man... that caller did this. She quickly turns towards her neighbor's house. Oh no. What about Mrs. Gregory?*

Chapter 11

Unwrapped

For the first time in her adult life, Brooke feels helpless. As she sits on her front porch, everything around her is spiraling in an uncontrolled fashion, as if it waits for her to intercede.

The ambulance has long gone. Mr. Gregory is on his way to that cold and unrelenting place to pause before he can finally be laid to rest. Mrs. Gregory is completely torn apart. Forty-six years of marriage has ended without any warning or prejudice. Her sister and brother-in-law are helping her grieve through this most unfortunate circumstance.

The police suspected no foul play, so Brooke's house is not held hostage to a crime scene. There is measured concern over the phone conversation she reported. They believe Brooke might have an overzealous observer, who just happened to be at the right place and the right time when Mr. Gregory expired.

"Miss Hannah, we have combed the immediate area surrounding your home and have found nothing to be suspect." said the policeman. "We also checked your doors and locks. Everything is operational without anything being compromised.

"As far as the caller, you may potentially have a stalker. Your face is easily recognizable; however, your private life is not. If I were you, I would be extra vigilant when coming home at night and leaving out in the early morning hours. It's helpful that you have an attached garage. If you already don't, get in the habit of backing your car in. You want to create as many vantage points as possible.

"I'm not sure how he got your cell phone number; however, in this day of data hacking and security breaches, it may not be that difficult anymore. If you come down to the station and file a formal complaint, we can have your provider pull your cell phone records and track that loser down."

"Thank you, officer. I am hoping this was an isolated incident. Maybe he got scared off for good when I dialed 911. If I get any more phone calls, I will be sure to file an official complaint. I'm still a bit confused. How do you think Mr. Gregory ended up on my porch? Did you see the front of his clothes? He had fresh grass stains and dirt on his pants and shirt."

"Based on what you told me about the previous night, I'm assuming he was trying to make some more tea and became confused with his surroundings. As he walked over to your house, he probably slipped and fell. Once he recovered himself, he probably decided to sit for a spell on your swing. In his last moments, he wanted something serene. He died where he found it."

"But what about the teapot? It's fragile glass. Surely if he fell, the teapot should have shattered, right?"

"I won't deny you bring up a valid point. Judging by the way he was holding it in his lap, I would say he was protecting it. In his last moments, that teapot and that swing are all that mattered. I do believe it is as simple as that. I'm sorry for the loss of your neighbor, Miss Hannah. From speaking with his wife, I can see he was a really nice man. I want you to take my card. If you have any problems, please don't hesitate to call me. Try and get some rest."

As the officers' leave, there is no sense of normalcy for Brooke. Sleep is the last thing that she'd be able to realize on this odd and extremely sad night. She hopes that she never speaks with the strange caller again. But deep down, she knows it's only a matter of time.

Chapter 12

Clear Expectations

May 12, 2015

It has been another busy and productive day at work, as Brooke drives home to change before heading to the Cancer Fighter's Charity Ball.

Her Bluetooth headset vibrates as she answers the phone without regard to her caller id.

"Hello this is Brooke. Hold on for just a minute while I let these windows up... OK, thank you for holding."

"Hello Brooke, it's nice to hear your voice again," said the man.

Brooke is immediately panicked. She would never forget that voice.

"Listen, whoever you are I'm placing you on notice that the police have already been informed about you. They will be tracking this number..."

"*STOP!* Allow me to be very clear with you, Miss Hannah. You can have the entire police department comb through your precious call records. They will never find anything to aide them in their search. You can have them trace my call, and they will come up empty-handed and confused.

"Sure, the police will have to be involved in this business between you and me at some point. But at no time will you ever go to them directly for help without my express consent. Your non-conformance or non-compliance will result in pain unimaginable. Now, that was my quick spiel, more details are forthcoming. Trust me when I say I know all I need to know about you and can push any button I want. By the way, my condolences for your dearly departed neighbor."

Brooke is too shaken to continue driving as she pulls off to the shoulder of the highway.

"You did it. You killed Mr. Gregory. How could you? Why are you doing this? Who are you?"

"You have no idea how misaligned and offensive your accusation is. You will learn very soon how I operate, and you will respect the precision in which I do things. To bring some peace to your mind, I did not kill your precious tea drinker. I admit I was watching you from afar when low and behold guess what I saw? Mr. Gregory treading his way towards your house. He made it about halfway before he dropped to his knees, in I swear, the slowest manner possible. I was deeply touched by the way he protected that teapot. He gently set it down at his side before collapsing flat on his face.

"I couldn't believe what I had witnessed. Really it was touching. The wheels in my mind are always turning I swear. I decided to drive over and bring Mr. Gregory to his original destination. I'm hoping you enjoyed the gesture of placing him in your swing. And there is no way you can deny the elegant touch of placing that teapot in his lap. In the end, it seemed like that mattered the most."

Brooke has to quickly collect herself. This is not a caller who's just going to hang up. He has a purpose, and he intends to let her know how she fits into the equation.

"Tell me what it is that you want? You obviously know a lot about me. Why are you contacting me?"

"That is a rather difficult question to answer over the phone; however, you are nowhere near ready to meet me. This Friday at 7:00pm you need to be at the intersection of 93 and I-275. You will be surrounded by daylight, cars, and people. Someone will stand out amongst them all. They will give you a key. The key goes to a P.O Box inside the post office on Bessie Coleman Blvd. I'm sure you'll be able to find it. The contents of the box will give you some additional clarity."

"Listen, I don't know who you are, but I'm not going to a P.O. Box or meeting anyone anywhere. And do you realize you're asking me to meet someone in the intersection of two freeways? Whatever you need to say to me will have to be done over the phone."

"Brooke, You Are Testing My Patience. If you are not there as instructed, my next visit will be to someone near and dear to you. I will video record and show you how creative I can be with simple needle and thread. You *don't* want me to have to be that guy. 7:00pm Friday. Six times three equals nine… Goodbye."

Brooke remains on the side of the road, reduced to tears.

Why are you doing this to me? I don't understand what this is you're doing. Lord help me please. I don't know what to do.

If it's one thing that she knows, it's not involving anyone from the police department, though her training tells her otherwise. She realizes she's going to have to play his game until she can understand his angle. She also realizes that she may be putting her life in danger.

Chapter 13

The Key to Understanding

Three days later

I don't want to sound like a broken record but are you sure everything is ok?" asked Charlie as he puts away his equipment in the news van. "You've been focused on the world of outer space for most of the day. And if you look at that watch again, I'm going to lose it."

"Yes, Charlie, I'm fine. You are such a worry wart. I'm just a little flustered thinking about all the things I want to get done this weekend."

"OK, but you know all you have to do is ask and I'll be there. Oh, and Lori and I don't have a lot planned. We will gladly drop by and help you out."

"As usual, you are incredibly sweet. You are my rock, I swear. But I'll be fine, I promise. Besides, we are about to officially kick the weekend off, right? Let's do it!"

6:59pm

This makes absolutely no sense. Am I supposed to just stop in the middle of the freeway?

"OH GOD, that can't be."

Just beyond Brooke's vision she can see something coming up on her right-hand side. As she gets closer, she sees it's a woman walking down the embankment of the freeway.

What is she doing? She's about to walk onto the freeway.

With each step the woman takes, it appears she may fall. She is off-balance and disjointed. Her chin is tucked, as her disheveled blond hair completely covers her face. Cars continue to race by with little regard for what they've just witnessed. Some of them are even rude enough to blow their horns in delightful fashion.

The woman suddenly stops and looks to her left as Brooke pulls up on the shoulder. The woman plops down on the grassy hill. Brooke runs up to her.

"Hello, are you OK? My name is Brooke and I'm going to help you. Are your hurt? What's your name?"

Brooke can't help but notice the condition that the woman is in. She is wearing a long white sundress that's quite dirty. By the way she smells, it's obvious she's being wearing this for quite some time. Her hands are tucked beneath her, and she is wearing terribly soiled white sweat socks, as she rocks gently back and forth. Brooke attempts to touch her face, but the woman woefully rejects.

"I'm going to get you some help. I think you need to see a doctor. Where were you coming from?"

As Brooke takes out her phone the woman looks up at her. Her hair still covering her face in arranged disillusion. She reaches between her legs.

"What are you doing? Please wait, don't do anything. I'm going to get you help. Are you pregnant?"

The woman lets out a muffled whimper, as if she purposely keeps her mouth closed. She pulls her hand from between her legs. Her fingers are covered in blood. She takes the small object in her hand and wipes it off on her dress, as she unemotionally smears blood.

She raises her hand and between her fingers is a key.

"Dear Lord, it's you!? You are the person I'm supposed to meet? This is sick, I have to get you some help."

The woman strongly motions with her hand for Brooke to take the key. Reluctantly, Brooke takes it and places it in her purse.

Her phone rings. She quickly grabs it knowing it's *him* on the other end. She answers without saying a word.

"Six times three equals nine. Mama, give me a chance. I know how to do it." said the man in a panicked voice.

Brooke looks at her phone confusedly.

"I think it would be a good time to call an ambulance for our young friend. You better hurry."

The man terminates the call. The woman lays on her side curling up as if she were taking a nap. You can see the flow of blood arched and canvassing from where she pulled the key.

"Please hold on. I'm getting you some help right now. Please hold on. We must find out why he did this. You have to live. Please…"

Chapter 14

Haven't We Met?

The traffic along I-275 through this stretch of St. Petersburg has been reduced to crawling speeds. The police have closed down all but one lane as they continue their investigation of this bizarre event.

Brooke is shaken and paranoid. She has the blood-stained key in her purse and knows her next destination. She is convinced she is dealing with a maniac. He will obviously resort to anything to get his point across; though, it's still unclear what kind of game he's playing and how she's involved.

Brooke prays for the survival of the woman. She might be the one person who can end this sick ordeal. She wonders what horrors this woman had to endure. The only thing remotely normal on this day, is the face and half-smile that approaches her.

"Haven't we met?" said the officer and he extends his hand.

"It's nice to see you again officer, just not under these circumstances. I apologize I never looked at your business card. Your name is?"

"Detective Engler is the name. And no worries. You went through a lot that night. From the looks of it today, you were at the right place at the right time, though, that might be argued. There's nothing more that can be done here. They are going to do all they can to save her. We're not far from the station. Can you join me there? We can talk with more privacy."

Before she can reply her cell phone rings. She drops her purse on the ground stricken with fear. She quickly recomposes herself.

"I'm sorry, I need to take this." gestured Brooke to the detective. "I will meet you at the station within an hour if that's ok."

"Sure, that works. Thank you, and I will see you there."

"Hello Mr. Bergdoll."

She is completely relieved to have someone else on her phone.

"Brooke, my goodness are you ok?"

"Yes sir, I'm doing just fine. A little shaken up right now, but I'm more concerned about that woman. I've never experienced anything like that."

"Brooke, something truly unprecedented has happened. In my career I have never seen anything like this. The other news channels are staying away from this one. They are providing some cursory coverage but that's about it. I believe the level of respect for you and this situation is quite high. I hate to do this, but I need you to give an exclusive. I don't need you to win an Emmy, just give some quick facts. In and out. Charlie will be there by the time we end this phone conversation. This is going to be our breaking news story."

"I understand sir. I see Charlie now. We will do a quick patch in right away."

"Thank you, Brooke. I want you to take an extra day this weekend. No worries, ok? I will see you on Tuesday. Don't hesitate to call me if you need anything."

"Yes sir. I appreciate the generosity. We will be live in less than five minutes."

As she has done so many times, Brooke lights up the camera with poise, intelligence, and conviction. She gives the facts of the story obviously leaving out the details of the key, and the true purpose behind her being there.

Before she can meet with the detective, she will first needed to visit the P.O. Box. She has no idea what awaits her.

Chapter 15

Believable Story

As Brooke pulls up to a nearly empty parking lot of the post office, she quickly scans her surroundings. The defensive side of her says this is some type of set up. The logical side of her knows that such a thing wouldn't flow well in this story this unknown person is stringing together.

As fortune would have it, a family pulls up beside her, and a man exits the vehicle to head inside. Brooke quickly follows suit, using this opportunity as a safety net. She removes the key from her purse with the small white cloth that it lay on top of.

The key has a number of 23123. Brooke looks up at the directional areas in the P.O. Box section and finds the location with ease. She peers to her right in comfort seeing the man that had come in before her was reading his mail on the table.

She opens the mid-sized box and retrieves a small 5x7 padded yellow envelope. She quickly closes back the box and exits ahead of the man still reading his mail. She doesn't feel safe in the parking lot, even with the family present. She exits and makes her way to the police station to meet with Detective Engler. She would have to view the contents later.

St. Petersburg Police Department

As Brooke sits down in Detective Engler's office, she realizes that much of what she will be saying will be scripted.

This is unfamiliar territory for Brooke, as she has always been above board, just as her dad had taught her. She knows she has to throw the detective off any semblance of a scent.

"Miss Hannah, I really appreciate you dropping by to give your statement." said the detective. "I was trying to save you from doing what you ended up having to do. I must say your breaking news persona was not the least bit frazzled. I also know your time is quite valuable so let's begin. But just one more thing, Miss Hannah. This one has been sitting on my mind. I didn't think our paths would cross again, so I sorta buried it.

"In the spirit of full disclosure, I was not supposed to be at your house that night when Mr. Gregory passed away. It just so happened I was literally three minutes away from you when I heard the call over the radio. When I heard it was you, I decided to respond immediately. But don't worry ma'am... it was for purely professional reasons and nothing more."

"Well, I certainly appreciate your candor, detective. Full disclosure up front is always reassuring."

"Agreed. So, Miss Hannah, walk me through how you discovered this young lady."

"Well, I had a taste for Cracker Barrel and decided to dine in. I was heading down 93 just before the merge with I-275 when I saw something odd up on my right. This lady was walking down the hill, almost like sleep walking. I thought she was going to walk onto the freeway when she suddenly plopped down on the grass. I pulled over and ran up to her. Her hair was in her face the whole time. She wouldn't let me touch her. She also wouldn't speak. She just sat on her hands rocking back and forth. Then she just lied down on her side in a fetal position. That's when I called 911. She never responded to me."

"So, you never saw her hands or face?"

"Correct, she acted very reclusive."

The detective's phone rings, startling Brooke again.

"I'm sorry Miss Hannah, I need to grab this. Detective Engler speaking. I see. Well, thank you for the phone call. Damn good work today.

"Miss Hannah, that was one of my men calling from the hospital. The woman you were trying to help didn't make it. I'm sorry."

Brooke is shaken hearing the news.

"Who was she?"

"Her name was Ingrid Sellers. She was reported missing last month. She was a county clerk from Tampa. Her family has already been notified."

"That poor girl."

Brooke's stomach sinks even further.

"Listen Miss Hannah, there's something I need to tell you about Ingrid. Something it appears you were completely oblivious to. When the paramedics arrived and began to examine her, they made a grisly discovery. Her mouth and eyes were both sewn completely shut by needle and thread. That's probably why she refused to clear the hair out of her face. That also explains why she couldn't talk to you. But there's more. All the fingers on her right hand, and three of her fingers on her left were also completely sewn together. They resembled one-piece mittens. Why her left hand was different than the right is unclear at this point. Her toes on both her feet were in the same manner, only no difference between left and right."

Brooke quickly thinks about the woman reaching between her legs and giving her the key. But her fingers were covered in blood, she simply didn't notice what the detective is describing. There is a knot developing in her stomach, as she is starting to feel ill.

"Should I stop? I apologize, I know this is gruesome."

"There's more!?" Brooke is mortified. "No. I'll be fine, please continue, detective."

"She had the arm of baby doll lodged inside her vagina. It was completely covered with small ultra-fine needles. It completely tore her up inside. That's the reason behind you seeing all the blood from her lower half. That, and we believe she may have been pregnant. Those results are still inconclusive.

"Miss Hannah, I need to ask you a favor, person to person, leaving our professional obligations out of this one. No one from the media knows any of this except you. We'd like to keep it that way. Rest assured we are going to find the sick bastard that did this to that poor young lady. Can I get a commitment from you?"

"Detective, I will not divulge any parts of this conversation. You have my word."

"Thank you, that means a lot. We just don't need the other pressures interfering with this investigation at this point. When our needs change, I would like to personally reach out to you if that's OK."

"Absolutely detective. I am here to help in any way I can. If that's all, I would really like to get some fresh air now. I need to detox my brain."

"By all means. We are all done here. Thank you again for dropping by. Oh, there was something else. Have you gotten anymore strange phone calls?"

Brooke smiles and carefully replies.

"Not since that night, detective. I think your crew did a nice job of scaring him off for good. Please enjoy your evening."

As Brooke leaves the police station, the outside air quickly dispatched the nauseous feeling. She cringes as she sees the padded envelope on the passenger seat of her car. This game has turned deadly and psychotic. She is completely overwhelmed with what her role is in this twisted equation. She is also still quite disparate over the brutality that fell Ingrid Sellers. There is no way she can wrap her mind around what type of person could do such a thing. There's one person that can soothe her mind. And right now, she needed him more than ever.

Chapter 16

Parental Guidance

Brooke decides to take no chances with opening the padded envelope. She stops by the local hardware store and purchases disposable gloves, eye protection, and a mask for her nose and mouth. She knows she can ill afford to make any mistakes.

As she arrives home, she remembers Detective Engler's advice and backs her car up the driveway and into the garage. She is supremely vigilant and aware of her surroundings. Before she delves into the unknown, she decides to call her dad. No matter the situation, his voice has always brought her comfort.

"Hi dad, how are you doing? What are you up to? Where's mom?"

"Well hello sweetie. I'm winding down, I suppose. I figured I'd do a little reading before bed. Your mom is in the other room catching up on some things she recorded last week. How are you doing? Is everything OK? You don't normally call this late."

There is silence on the line, as Brooke tries to keep it together. The other thing about her dad, other than his voice, is the sense of peace and calm he has always projected. Surely these are the two things that Brooke sorely lacks right now.

"Honey, what's wrong?

He knows his daughter quite well, and can sense when she's distraught.

"Take your time, I'm here for you."

"Dad, I'm sorry." she said as she breaks into tears. "It's just... I really miss you and mom sometimes. And I guess right now I'm just a little overwhelmed. I wish I was at home."

"Oh no darling. Why are you overwhelmed? Is it the job?"

"Yes, kind of, dad. There's just so much going on right now. I can't seem to see straight. I'm sorry for calling you with this. I just wanted to hear your voice that's all."

"No baby, never apologize. I am here for you always. Your mother and I love you dearly. So, tell me, have you at least identified or narrowed down the source for what's making you feel this way?"

That question is an easy one to answer for Brooke. All her frustration revolves around the phone call from that night. She wonders if she was somehow randomly chosen. That it was just her bad luck she decided to answer. Regrettably, these were not scenarios she could bounce off her dad for obvious reasons.

"Listen dad, I'm working on something highly confidential. This is currently the source of the stress right now. I might not be able to talk to you and mom as often as I was. It should be temporary though. I think everything will be back to normal soon."

"Brooke, do you remember Mr. Rabbit?"

Brooke smiles.

"Mr. Rabbit!? Yes, dad, I remember him. My very first pet. I wanted a rabbit but got a puppy instead. You and mom told me

I could name him Mr. Rabbit. I knew something like this was coming."

She starts to lighten up.

"When we were getting ready to head down south to visit your grandmother, you wanted to have a conversation with Mr. Rabbit. You thought your mom and I were outside, but I was just outside your door. You told him that you were leaving for a little while, but that you'd be back. You told him not to worry or be scared, because he would always be protected. You picked him up while his little tail wagged and told him that you loved him.

"You know what? You kept your word. You took great care of Mr. Rabbit up till the time we had to put him to sleep. And do you remember what you told him as you said goodbye? You said, don't be afraid, we'll be together forever.

"Brooke, whether you are near or far, whether it's cloudy or sunny, you can depend on me and your mom to always be there for you. Whatever you are going through right now, please remember that you are *going through it,* not staying it. Follow that advice you gave to Mr. Rabbit a long time ago and be brave. Face it and don't let it stare you down. You will always be kinder, wiser, and more resourceful. Now go tear down that problem, baby."

"Dad, I don't know how you do it, but you can always make my face twist up into a smile. I really needed this. Thank you, dad, I love you."

The phone call gave Brooke the dose of sanity that she needed to face this nightmare.

And now to find out what's inside that envelope.

H. Eugene

Chapter 17

Flash of Knowledge

Brooke realizes she won't be able to sleep unless she opens the envelope tonight. She readies her gear, likening herself to an ER Surgeon. She carefully opens the envelope and dumps the contents onto the kitchen table.

It is a small flash drive and a small index card. She reads the card:

"I'm sure you've had a long day. Why don't you load that flash drive up tomorrow? I need you to be fully energized. 6x3=9"

Milk

Milk!? That's your name? What kind of... and why do you keep saying that ridiculous math equation. It doesn't make any sense. So, you know my every move, is that it? Are you watching me right now?

The next morning

Brooke normally wakes up each morning without the aid of an alarm clock at 6:00am. But today she sleeps till nearly 8:00am. The activities from the previous day not only drained her body, but also her mind. There is no time for rest or reluctance. She needs to know what's on that flash drive. She wonders if the answers are only the beginning of this bad dream she's been thrust into.

After a quick shower and breakfast, she places the flash drive into her desktop as she peers out the window in her home office. Paranoia has officially settled in. As she opens the flash drive.

Password? Are you serious right now? How would I have the password?

She grabs the envelope and index card that accompanied the flash drive to search for clues.

This is a game, Brooke. Come on, think girl think.

She decides to try something that she knows would be too easy. she enters her first name in lowercase letters.

Bingo! Wow it worked. I can't believe it worked.

Once opened, there is one file folder on the flash drive. As she clicks to open, there is only one additional file, a video. She proceeds to watch with intrigue.

The video is shot in full HD, so the details are all very crisp. There is a camera panning a room. There are no images, and the room seems barren. The point of view changes to another camera that slowly scrolls up from a transfixed position on the floor. As the camera slowly raises its' tilt, a disturbing image presents itself.

Are those people? What is this?

Brooke looks on in disgust and horror.

As the camera continues to pan, she can see someone attached to a metal peg board. Their hands and feet are completely spread apart like they were making a snow angel image. It's difficult to tell from the video; however, they must be bound to this wall in some way. They are unable to move. There is a straw sack pulled over their head. Based on the body features, you can distinguish that it's a male.

The camera cuts out for a moment. When it reappears, there is a man standing in front of a white wall. As the camera pans back, you can see writing on each of the three walls in the camera's line of sight.

The camera zooms in just behind the man dressed in a black cap and gown. He is writing something on the wall in black marker. As the camera continues to move over his shoulder and shows a close up of the wall, he was writing 6 x 3 = 9. In fact, that's what the entire wall says. As the camera zooms backward to a position just behind the man, Brooke moves her face closer to the screen.

What is this? It's all over the wall. He has written the same math equation all over the wall. I don't understand this.

The camera cuts off again. When it comes back online, it shows just the wall the man was writing on. An audio clip starts.

"You will know the truth. Once you know it, you will either provide the solution, or I will do so myself. Now it's time to put those college degrees to work. I hope you can figure everything out. Six times three equals nine!"

What am I supposed to do with this? He has someone there. He has a hostage. Keep it together. No tears Brooke. No more crying. Figure it out girl. You can do this. Someone needs me. I don't understand the math equation. Surely, he believes its right, but why?

While Brooke contemplates her next move, so does the psychopath.

Chapter 18

Motivational Speech

May 19th 2015

"This country was not founded by wise men." stated the speaker.

He looks out of the window of his classroom. There is an oversized chalkboard on the wall beside him. The desks are made like those in an elementary school but sized for adults. He continues.

"This country was founded by opportunists who enslaved our minds with reproductive propaganda. You don't make it in this world. You simply provide the resources that enable the entitled a continuous degree of measured control. Every time you read a book or open your mouth to speak, poison formulates and spews. Your minds are poisoned by the promise. The reality will never manifest itself until you free yourself from the cascading virtues.

"What am I doing? I'm just wasting my breath on the uninitiated. As I continue to speak, I'm also beginning to feel dumber. Thank you for completely taking advantage of my precious time. OK, let's do something simpler for the lesser minds. I think it's a great time to role-play." He points across the room. "And the first sheep said?"

"I am number one." replied the woman. "My shape is square."

"I am number two." said another woman. "My shape is round."

"I am number three." said the man. "My shape is rectangular."

There is a prolonged silence as the speaker stares.

"I'm not doing this." remarked the other man sharply. "I want to leave this damn place. This is wrong what you are doing."

"There's always someone that wants to ruin it for everyone else. Everyone, look at the man without a number and a shape. Study him well. This is the type of person I was alluding to at the beginning of my speech. As we try to overcome the chains that try to bind us, he tries to make them heavier and tighter.

"If you don't read your damn script with precision, I'm going to gut you like a pig and have your three neighbors eat your intestines while you watch. Do I Make Myself Crystal Clear? No mama, I can do it. I promise, I can do it. Please don't hurt me. It burns so bad, mama."

There is brief, yet uncomfortable silence. No one dares look at the other. If they do what he says to the letter, he'll calm down. A voice suddenly crumbles.

"I am number four, my shape is triangular." said the man.

He knows the speaker meant every word he said.

"I told you I could do it mama." said the speaker.

He is still delusional and talking to himself. Quickly he returns to his *normal* self and smiles.

"Very good. Please accept my apologies for using my big voice. You all are quick learners. The role-play was quite impressive. My lesson plan for today revolves around making personal sacrifices or having them made for you. I need each of you to open your desk drawers and remove the clear plastic container. Place it directly on the desk in front of you. Number one, please tell the class what's in your container."

"It's a pair of rusted hair clippers and a sentence on a post-it note."

"Number two, what's in your container?"

"I have a pair of tweezers and a sentence on a post-it note."

"And what about you, number three? What's in your container?

"It's a small pack of burn cream, and a sentence on a post-it note."

"Very good. And how about you, number four? We saved the best for last. What's in your container?"

"My container is empty."

The man looks confused.

"Well, today is indeed your lucky day, Mr. Triangle. Here's what happens now. Number one, those hair clippers are going to shave your head bald, and I mean baby clean. Number two, those tweezers are to pluck all the hairs from your left eyelash. And I want the full strands plucked one by one. Number three, you're going to need that burn cream when the boiling water from that coffee pot on the burner is poured on the lower half of your left arm and hand. And guess what number four does? Well, you get to administer each task while they sit there and take it. When I return, you will each need to read the sentence individually chosen for you aloud.

"This is what I meant by personal sacrifice. Now, I'm going to go and freshen up a bit. I will return in one hour. If

67

everything is not completed as I asked, I will do it myself. And please know I won't be careful. And number four, if I end up disappointed, I'm going to revisit what I had to threaten you with for your intolerance not long ago. I hope I have made myself perfectly clear. I will not entertain any questions. I'll be back folks."

Chapter 19

Reading Between the Lines

May 20, 2015

Nice job with your speech today Brooke," said Charlie. "You really got those seniors fired up. I think this is one of the better career days we've done, wouldn't you agree?"

"Yes, I totally agree. The students were engaged from the very beginning. They were quite respectful of all the speakers. It's a shame this is an exception versus the norm."

"You got that right. I know I'm going to get the look for asking you this."

"Well, that probably means you shouldn't ask, Charlie."

"Is everything still going ok? I know I asked you before, but you just seem different these past couple of weeks."

Brooke gives him a genuine smile.

"And you ask anyway. There are some things that have me preoccupied right now. But I promise they will be over soon. OK?"

"OK, fair enough. You know what you need this evening?"

"What do I need, ole wise one?"

"A glass of Merlot and a good book. Nothing too heavy though. Something to relax your mind."

Brooke looks at Charlie like he just said the best thing she has ever heard.

"Charlie, my goodness, you are a genius. Why didn't I think of that? That's exactly what I'm going to do. Thank you."

"Are you being funny or serious?"

"No, very serious right now. There is something I've been putting off reading. Tonight, is the perfect time.

6:45pm

As Brooke arrives home, she's been playing a scenario through in her head. She's hoping that scenario will be confirmed. She grabs the copy of the book, *Of Mice and Men* given to her by Thaddeus Gainsborough. She turns the book down to the floor and flips through the pages like she was shuffling a deck of cards, hoping for something to fall out but to no avail.

OK, I guess I'll just read this darn book after all.

As she sits back and starts reading, something captures her attention on page 14. The first letter of two different words is circled. As she flips the page, there are more letters circled in no particular pattern.

Hey wait a minute. I need to write these down. This has to be spelling out something.

As she continues to scroll through the pages, more letters are circled. She continues to write them down not paying attention to what they might be saying. Sometimes pages or entire chapters are skipped before the circling of letters continues. Finally, she reaches the end of the book, to her surprise. She studies her notebook looking for a pattern, having written down each letter in the order that she saw them.

u n D e R T H E b E D r E M O v T h e R a I S n W o O d

Under the bed remove the raisin wood? What bed is he referring to, and what is raisin wood? Hey wait a minute. I wonder if what he's referring to is inside of the house they found him. I need to get access to that house. I know just the person to call. I know he will help me.

One of the most important things that Brooke has done since joining the Bay 9 News Team, is building great working relationships and powerful connections within many industries, more especially the various police departments. She decides to reach out to Chief Jared to ask for some assistance.

"Well, well! I know this number and have it saved," said the chief. "How are you doing, Brooke?"

"Hello chief, I am doing well. Please accept my apologies for calling at such a late hour."

"There is no worry at all. I am always glad to help. So, what can I do for you this evening?

"Sir, is it possible that I can visit Thaddeus Gainsborough's old residence? After interviewing him, I'd like to just provide some closure to myself with this story."

The chief pauses. "Are you sure you want to do that Brooke? That house is in the same condition as we found it in. Nothing has been cleaned up. There's a petition in place by the victim's families to have that place torn down. The house sits on a rather nice horse farm. It's on just over twenty acres of land. That son of a gun was quite loaded. With the discretion of having all that land, no one ever saw anything out of the ordinary. This is an unusual request. If you are sure you really want to go in there, I don't believe there'd be any issues. How quickly did you want to visit?"

"How about tomorrow morning or afternoon? I wouldn't need much time in there. Probably 10-15 minutes tops."

"OK, I will arrange to have one of my men meet you at the house. Let's do it in the morning, say around 9:30am?"

"That sounds perfect, chief. I really appreciate your help with this."

"Not at all Brooke. My department and I owe you a debt of gratitude for always sticking with us versus sticking it to us like many of your colleagues. Enjoy the rest of your night."

"Please do the same, chief. Thank you!"

As Brooke leans back in her chair, she realizes she has to come to grips with the fact that Thaddeus Gainsborough has never completely left her head. She needs closure with this scenario, so she can focus all her time and energy into the current psychopath. This will also give her the opportunity to look at and study the surroundings. Perhaps this would give her some clues on the insight of a madman. This may be the type of research she needs to release her from this unbelievable script that someone has written.

Chapter 20

House Broken

The next morning Brooke meets with the policeman in his unmarked car at the news station. She follows him to the estate in the heart of the New Tampa area. Brooke is fascinated at how beautiful the property is, as they drive through the entrance gate. The land is still well manicured yet desolate without the horses. They arrive at the front entrance of the house. The officer opens his trunk.

"Miss Hannah, I believe the chief explained that this house is still in the same condition as the day Gainsborough was arrested. I imagine we're going to need these."

He reaches into the trunk and retrieves two facial masks, giving one to Brooke.

"Thank you, officer. Do you think it's safe to just go in?"

"I was going to suggest I go in first and look around. This is highly unusual to have someone canvassing an active crime scene, but if the chief's good, then so am I. I will come back out in a few moments and give you an all clear."

The officer removes the crime scene tape from around the door and enters the house. After a few short but tense moments he returns.

"Miss Hannah, the area is clear but I'm not sure you really want to go in there. The smell even with this mask on is nearly unbearable. And although the house has electricity, the central air isn't working. That just makes the smell a hundred times worse. But if you think you really want to go in, let's do it!"

"If you don't mind officer, I'd like to go in by myself. I won't be any longer than fifteen minutes. I just need to place myself in a zone and absorb the surroundings of this house. This is how I do my best reporting."

"Well, suit yourself, ma'am. I'm not sure how long you're going to be able to absorb anything past that smell. I'll sit just outside here and have a smoke if you don't mind?"

"Yes of course. I won't be long"

Brooke enters the house and is immediately overcome with nauseous fumes. The interior of the house was in excess of 90 degrees. She quickly reopens the front door.

"My God officer you were right. It is disgusting in here. I think I'll leave the front door open to get some fresh air in here."

"And I think I'll move closer to my car to enjoy my smoke. It's kinda funny that the quality of air from my cigarette smoke is a helluva lot better than what's inside there."

Brooke smiles and goes back into the house. As she looks around, the house is contemporarily styled and minimalist, with very little furniture present. The house is filled with varying types of cactus plants. Brooke thinks to herself that these are the only things that could survive in this place. The hardwood floors throughout gleam with a falsified innocence. As she passes an open door on the left, the smells escalates.

"Ugh! This must be the basement. Why didn't you close this door back?"

She yelled back to the officer, knowing he wouldn't hear her. She quickly closes it, knowing whatever evil occurred, happened in the basement.

OK so you said under the bed remove the raisin wood. Now, I just have to figure out which room is yours.

As she moves past the dining room, she enters the hallway. Just past it are two bedrooms on the left and a larger one on the right. As she enters the room on the right.

Bingo! I'm going to have to assume the cowboy hat hanging on the bed post with the initials T.G. belong to you Thaddeus.

Her brief sense of relief of finding his room is quickly dispatched by fear, as reality sets in that she is in the room of a psychopath.

Let's get this over with so I can get the hell out of here.

Brooke kneels on the wooden floor and cautiously looks beneath the bed. She rises to open the blinds to bring more light into the room. She returns and looks beneath the bed.

Under the bed remove the raisin wood. What the hell is raisin wood? There's nothing under here... what a minute! Are those raisins spilled under the bed?

"Miss Hannah, you ok in there?" Asked the officer through the front door.

"Everything but my heart." she yelled. "Geez, you scared the crap out of me. Yes, I'm fine!"

"Sorry, ma'am. OK, I'm just outside if you need me."

She peaks beneath the bed once more as her nerves are completely shot.

OK I see raisins. That's what you were referring to? Come on, talk to me Thaddeus.

She rises and gently moves the bed towards the wall, exposing the spilled raisins on the floor. As she walks up closer to inspect.

Hey, the floor is different here. It's hollow!

She quietly pats her feet around the area where the floor is hollow. There is a somewhat obvious hairline crack right between the spilled raisins. She removes a metal fingernail file from her purse and gently pries into the crack.

No way is it this easy.

She pulls back one small plank in the floor. Just inside is a notebook and a leather-clad journal. Both are positioned neatly on their sides. She removes both, places them in her purse, and positions the plank back into the floor.

What are these Thaddeus? I will find out tonight.

She quickly moves the bed back into place and closes the blinds. She removes herself quickly from the house and feels like she just entered another world. The fresh air fills her lungs.

"Officer, I really appreciate what you've done. I think I've seen all that I need to. I couldn't stand much more of that smell."

As Brooke follows the officer from the house back to the main road, she is consumed by what Thaddeus has laid out for her.

I don't know what's in those journals Thaddeus, but I hope it rids my mind of this odd feeling about you.

Chapter 21

The Favorite Son

Brooke has anxiously traversed through the day for the point at which she'd be home and able to pour through Thaddeus' notebook and journal. She lays back on her sofa and for the first time visually inspects both. The notebook appears to be quite old. The pages have started to yellow. They have the stench of old newspapers. The leather journal appears almost new. The pages are in pristine condition. She decides to begin with the notebook.

February 16th, 1981

"~~I love you mama and dad~~ I hate you. I hate it when you make me say that. I don't love you. You don't love me. They didn't like the show today. Dad threw his empty beer bottle at me. My wrist hurts really bad. It's swollen. I'm so hungry."

February 2th, 1981

"Mama is really mad at me. It's been a whole week and they won't let me come downstairs. I hear them laughing and having fun. Why can't they be like that around me? At least I haven't been beaten this whole time. That burn mark is still on my face from her cigarette."

July 5th, 1981

"The fireworks sounded really nice last night. They are better than last years. I wonder if I'll be able to ever play with them."

September 17th, 1981

"This is the first time in a long time mama and dad liked my performance. I thought mom was going to hit me with the plate, but instead she gave me pie. Mama can cook really well."

As Brooke turns the page, there are no more entries, just pictures. Page after page of nothing but pictures.

I guess you decided to use this for your artwork, huh? These pictures aren't really telling me anything. Just different facial pictures. They all look really sad. Are these you? I wonder how old you were when you wrote these?

As Brooke sets the notebook down, a piece of folded paper falls out of it from the back of the book. The message says Stooges RIP.

What does this mean?

She is trying her best not to feel any remorse for Thaddeus. *What kind of performances did your parents have you doing? This is becoming stranger and stranger.*

She picks up the leather journal. The condition is much newer from the outside. She reads on …

October 11, 2010

"It is so gratifying to see how make-believe can turn into something that truly blossoms. I love you Bartholomew. You are my very best friend. We have certainly grown through a lot. I don't know how often I will enter in this journal. I hate these things. Maybe I'll just update some milestones or special events that occur.

March 17, 2011

"Me and Bartholomew got two more horses today and boy are they pretty. Now we have four. I think that's plenty for now."

March 24, 2011

"That bastard was mean to our horse. He didn't know how to ride as well as he said he could. This made Bartholomew angry. You don't hurt animals... EVER! The man's head probably didn't deserve to be bashed in though. Was there another way?"

November 19, 2012

"I haven't written anything is this journal in some time. It's just too much. I can't keep up anymore. The killings won't stop. It can't stop! I don't know what to do anymore. I wonder if I should find mom again. She'll know what to say. I wonder if she still hates me?"

December 12, 2012

"I know the solution. Why didn't I think of this before? The killing will end today!"

As Brooke continues to skim through the pages, the rest are all blank.

I guess this is when you turned yourself in?

There is something affixed to the very back of the journal.

Hey, what's this? A letter?

Taped to the page is an envelope made out to Thaddeus. The sender is Abigail Gainsborough. Her address is in Jacksonville.

Are you his mom?

She opens the letter and reads it. It's only a few sentences where Abigail tells him she's not mad anymore and asks him to come and visit.

So, you saw your son during the time he was committing these murders!? Maybe you can provide me with some closure. I'm coming to see you!

Chapter 22

Permission Slip

May 22, 2015 the next morning

"Good morning Brooke, come on in and have a seat," said Mr. Bergdoll. "You sounded quite animated over the phone. Are you going to widen my smile this morning?"

"Well--perhaps sir. It's about the Gainsborough interview I did last month."

"Gainsborough!? Well, what else is there to report? Everything went without a hitch with the lethal injection. There were the usual protests, but nothing out of the ordinary. What angle do you have?"

"During my debrief at the governor's mansion, you'll remember I mentioned that Gainsborough had left me a copy of the book... *Of Mice and Men*. He was somewhat adamant that I reread the story. I had already read this book twice during my earlier years and didn't want to expend the energy reading it again.

"Well, a couple of days ago I decided to read it. There's been something eating at me about that interview since that day. As I flipped through the book, guess what I discovered? He had scribed some sort of coded message. The message led me to the home where all of the murders took place. I took some personal time yesterday morning to follow up on this lead. Please forgive me sir for not announcing what my intentions were first. I wanted to make sure this wasn't some type of wild goose chase. Get this, Gainsborough had hidden two diaries under his bed in a concealed slat in the floor."

"Are you flippin kidding me, Brooke? What did they say?"

"Well, there were no bombshells in either of them. But one thing that seemed to resonate, especially in the first one that I read was the violent relationship he had with his mother, Abigail. He sounds like he was being conditioned at a very early age. Their relationship might have been the catalyst which lead to his destructive behavior.

"He kept an envelope that contained a letter from his mother. It looks to be in response from one that he sent her. In it, she said she wanted to see him. This letter and likely his subsequent visit all happened at the height of his murder spree. I don't know where this story can possibly lead, but I want to follow up on this lead."

"So, it looks like his mom was the matriarch psycho. Have you discussed this with the governor or chief?"

"No sir, I wanted to have the discussion with you first. I'm still not sure this will result in anything worth raising everyone's ire."

"Good call. I am quite curious how far you can get with this. Where does she stay?"

"She's in Jacksonville, sir. About a four-hour drive from here. I've also done the necessary due diligence and called in a couple of favors. The address is legit, and she is still currently a resident. She stays in a rather nice condo."

"I wonder who financed that condo. Something tells me there are some things hidden. Let's see if she will bring them to light for us. I don't want this to be a solo effort. Is Charlie going with you?"

"Well, you segued into my next question. I was going to ask if he could accompany me. We spoke first thing this morning."

"Yes, absolutely. When do you plan to go?"

"I would like to go this coming Monday. It will give me the opportunity to tie up a few loose ends. I believe Abigail is going to be full of surprises."

Chapter 23

Guest Purposes

May 24, 2015

You've all made me quite happy." said the speaker. "And number four, you handled yourself admirably. I'm sorry we couldn't do this sooner after all your hard work, but duty called me elsewhere.

"Let's have a quick roll call. You all know the routine. The only difference is that you need to state what wonderful things happened to you. And don't forget to add your sentence of admiration from the post-it notes after your accomplishments. Since you were my helper number four, there's no need to articulate."

There's a pause, yet desperation as each person looks down at their desk. They dare not look the speaker in his eyes, nor at each other.

"I am number one. My shape is square. I had all of my hair shaved off my head. Thank you for making me feel clean."

"I am number two." Said the woman.

She is still visibly shaken, with her eye still badly bruised and near swollen.

"My shape is round. I had all the hairs of my left eyelash individually plucked with tweezers. Thank you for giving me character."

"I am number three. My shape is rectangular. I had scalding hot water poured on my arm and hand. Thank you for helping me feel needed."

"And number four, Mr. Triangular, you were able to save your intestines." said the speaker. "Nice job indeed. Now let's continue our class for today. I can't have you sitting around here with soft minds.

"We talked about personal sacrifice, and you each completed an exercise that I hope extended your learning around the process. If we need to repeat the lesson for understanding, I am more than willing to come up with a different set of role plays."

"I think we have all learned our lesson of personal sacrifice." said number two, as she tries her best not to cry for fear of burning her wounded eye. "We don't need to revisit that lesson anymore."

"Bravo number two," said the speaker. "I really appreciate your initiative. Very well then... let's discuss your purpose for being here. Number one, what is your profession?"

"I'm a homemaker sir."

"How about you, number two?"

"I'm also a homemaker sir."

"And number three, your turn."

"I'm a stay-at-home dad, sir."

"And last but certainly not least, please tell us your profession number four."

"Like number three, I'm a stay-at-home dad, sir."

"So, it doesn't take a genius to see the common thread here. Now by a show of hands, if you have children, raise them high.

All four of his subjects raise their hands, though with reluctance.

"And yet another common thread. Seems like we have a very nice group of students here. OK keep your hands high in the air for my next question. By a show of hands, how many of you are good parents? And by good, I mean you spend quality time with your children. You read them stories, you walk them to school, you tuck them into bed, and most importantly, you've *never* lost your patience and hurt them."

Slowly, each of the four lowers their hand and looks down at their desk, but this time in shame.

"Let's see how many hands I have raised...... I count Zero. So, we have our third and most alarming common thread. You are all child abusers. Last year was a grand year for you all. Number one, you broke your son's arm in two places. Number two, that iron pan required your daughter to have metal screws in her wrist. Number three, you came home drunk and beat your wife and fractured your two-year old's ribs. Number four, Mr. Triangular... Your son spent three months in the hospital with multiple breaks after you pushed him down the stairs."

The speaker turns his back to the four and walks to the chalkboard. He starts writing swiftly as the chalk screams across the board with the same thing repeated... 6 x 3 = 9

He writes it over and over again, each time faster than the previous.

"Mama I'm Sorry," shouted the speaker as his voice is panicked and erratic. His voice sounds like that of a young child. "I won't mess up again, I promise. Please don't burn me again mama. Please! Please! I'm hungry mama and I'm thirsty. Don't lock me in there."

The four subjects are limp and despondent. They can do nothing but hope that whatever button was pushed, it doesn't result in more pain for any of them.

"Ok mama, I understand now. They are going to pay. I am going to make them pay. They don't deserve to be loved anymore, mama."

The speaker puts down the chalk and turns towards the subjects.

"I have a new lesson plan."

Chapter 24

Abigail

May 25, 2015

Brooke and Charlie are less than half-hour away from their destination. She has told him everything surrounding Thaddeus Gainsborough, between having to manage conference calls and emails. As much as she wanted to, she didn't bring up the other mess that is the most cause for her anxiety.

Charlie has been Brooke's best friend since she joined the Bay 9 team. Charlie and his wife have had her over numerous times for dinner, and they have traveled on vacation together. She is the proud Godmother to their 4-year-old son, CJ. Charlie has been Brooke's rock on numerous occasions. Without him knowing the full details, he is being her rock right now.

"Well Brooke, I guess everything makes sense now," said Charlie. "I thought there was something just a little off with you, but I decided not to pry. Besides, you told me whatever it was you were going through, was coming to an end soon. I must admit I'm floored by the backdrop of all of this. So, what are your gut feelings about his mom? Do you think she'll give us the time of day? Don't you think it's odd that her name has never come up in any news coverage?"

"Yeah, I've thought about that too. There is something strange that I can't put my finger on. As far as she goes, I wouldn't be surprised if she's this kind-hearted old lady that wants us to eat some pie with her. We never talked about this, but didn't you get this feeling about Thaddeus that he was more of a book nerd than a serial killer?"

"You know, Brooke, I did think about that on the ride back from the prison. He was mild mannered and easygoing. He was more like a golf buddy. I suppose that's what makes these guys even more nutty and dangerous. They can switch personas at the drop of a dime."

"Yeah, I suppose you're right. Well, let's see where this thing goes, Charlie."

Brooke and Charlie arrive at Abigail Gainsborough's condo and follows another vehicle into the gated community of the *Valencia,* which is on the border of Ponte Vedra and Jackson Beaches. They park in front of her first floor condo.

"Alright let's do this." said Brooke.

They exit the vehicle and approach the front door. Charlie has his camera in tow. Brooke rings the doorbell.

"Who is it?" asked a voice sharply from behind the door, catching Brooke slightly off guard.

"Hello, Mrs. Gainsborough, my name is Brooke Hannah. I'm a reporter with the Bay 9 News. I'd like a few moments of your time to ask you a few questions."

"*A reporter.* Well, I don't know what you want here. There's nothing you need to be asking me. Who sent you here?"

"Yes ma'am, I understand your apprehension. But I just wanted to ask you some questions about the Thaddeus Gainsborough case."

There is complete silence as Brooke clears her throat.

"Mrs. Gainsborough, are you still there?"

Still nothing but silence.

"OK Charlie, looks like I have to go with option B."

"Option B!? What's option B?" What are you about to do? I know that look in your eyes."

"Watch and learn, buddy boy."

Brooke rings the doorbell again.

"Mrs. Gainsborough, I know you can hear me. I promise I won't take up much of your time... I know Thaddeus was your son."

The door snatches open.

"You watch your tongue, miss. It's peaceful and quiet here. I don't need this monkey circus around here. What do you want from me? How do you know me?

"I'll gladly explain, Mrs. Gainsborough if you'll just let us inside. This is my camera technician, Charlie. Please, we don't mean to cause you any trouble."

Mrs. Gainsborough looks at Brooke and Charlie, studying them both carefully.

"OK come on in before my neighbors start getting too curious. But you can't bring that camera recorder or whatever it's called in here with you."

"Charlie, do you mind?" asked Brooke.

"Not at all. This seems like Déjà vu." He takes his video camera back out to the truck and returns back inside.

"I hope you don't mind me not offering you anything," said Mrs. Gainsborough. "I don't plan on you staying here very long. Well, have a seat over there."

She points to the sofa next to the window.

"So, I'm going to ask you again, how do you know about me? I have not had one reporter come by here... for anything."

"I interviewed your son by his request on the day of his execution. I believed he wanted to make peace with what he had done. He gave me a couple of diaries that he had been keeping. That's how I found out about you."

Mrs. Gainsborough is frantic.

"Diaries!? What do you mean? I never saw any diaries. Where are they?"

"I don't have them with me ma'am, but I can assure you they are in a safe place."

"Well since you're here because of these things he wrote, why don't you tell me what he said?"

"Well, he didn't say a lot ma'am, but the little bit that I read was quite powerful. He spoke about the abuse he received from you and his dad."

"Watch your tongue young lady. That's the last time I'm going to tell you that."

"I meant no disrespect, ma'am. I'm just relaying what he wrote about. He seemed to be quite lonely. So much so, that he created a pretend friend named Bartholomew. Did he ever mention this person to you?"

"I wanna set one thing straight, Miss Reporter. His dad and I treated him like a king. We never laid a hand on that boy. I don't like this insinuation that we were bad parents because that's what you're saying. We spent plenty time with him. I heard him talk about that name. It's like most little boys. Since he was the only child, he played make believe a lot. My little boy was beautiful, and he became a brilliant man. It's a shame that society has painted such an unfair picture of him."

"Mrs. Gainsborough, are you saying that you don't believe he killed all of those people?"

"My son was never a killer. You killed the wrong man. His blood is on your hands, Miss Fancy Reporter.

"Ma'am, I understand how hard this whole ordeal must be for you. Your son admitted in the diary that he was killing these people and that he didn't know how to stop. He even gave details on how one of the people died. It looks like he came to visit you not too long before he turned himself in. Can you tell me about that conversation?"

Mrs. Gainsborough looks bitter and resentful for the question that was just asked.

"I don't like your types, Miss Reporter. You two come in my home real uppity like. You probably think you're better than me, but you're not. How old are you girl?"

"I don't believe that has any relevance on…"

"How Old Are You?" Mrs. Gainsborough's voice escalates.

"I'm 28 Mrs. Gainsborough."

"I can look at you and tell you don't have any children. Hell, you've probably never been in love or had a man touch you. All those damn books you study have diluted your mind. There's only one person that can judge me, and that ain't you. So, what if my son came to visit me. Are you trying to say that I was some type of accomplice now?"

"No ma'am, that's not what I was trying to say. I would like to know what he discussed with you while he was here. Did he confess anything to you? Did you know then that he was responsible for those murders?"

"City girl didn't you hear what I told you the first time? For a reporter, you don't listen very well. My son was terribly misunderstood. He was no murderer. I don't care what you think. You've crucified my poor son. You all will pay for what you done.

"You need to burn those damned books you found. They are nothing but the devil. My husband passed away nearly two years ago. Thaddeus was his world. Kids play make believe a lot and say and write things that were all made up in their pretty heads. They do it all the time. Hell, even grown people do it.

"We both loved that boy dearly. If you try to take some garbage you found and smear my boy's good name, I will sue you. Not get out of here, the both of you. You're making my stomach upset."

"Very well, Mrs. Gainsborough. We really do appreciate your time. I apologize if I offended you in anyway."

"I'm not offended, I'm just a little sick right now. That smell of arrogance is making me dizzy. Goodbye, Miss Reporter!"

Brooke and Charlie exit and make their way back to the news truck.

"Wow, Brooke, can you believe that nut case? She is definitely hiding something."

"You may be right, Charlie. But what she may be hiding is nothing that will bring us anything fluid enough to report on. I believe she is delusional, but really loved her son. The diaries are strange still. I think it's time to lay this one to bed."

Although she is disappointed with the outcome of this visit, Brooke is satisfied that this brings her some type of closure. In this job, she has come across many varying personalities. Yet, she knows that she hasn't seen it all. Thaddeus, it seems, was looking for something quite simple, yet undervalued by many. He just wanted someone to talk to. Brooke realizes that was the whole of this entire exercise. He longed for friendship outside of his make believe one.

There were some lessons learned in playing this game with Thaddeus. But nothing could prepare her for what came next.

Chapter 25

Stained Doves

The next morning

Brooke is wide awake in her bed as she stares at the ceiling fan's blades rotate and justify a fainted breeze. She grabs her cell phone off the other pillow to look at the time.

OK, it's too early to get up. Close your eyes and just relax. It's going to be a busy.

Her phone rings, nearly making her jump from her bed. It's not an unknown caller like previous time when he called.

It's 3:45 in the morning. If this is some drunk moron with the wrong number

"Hello!"

"Hello, Brooke, It's very nice to hear your voice again. I couldn't sleep and needed a special friend to call," said the man as Brooke's heart races.

"The number that came up on your caller id is my personal cell phone. The number can't be traced, so don't bother. But please, I want you to use this as a means to get in contact with me anytime you'd like to talk. I'm a great listener."

"What do you want?" Brooke said demandingly, though with a measure of constraint.

"I need you to pull up a website. There's something I want you to see."

"And there was no way you could have waited to call me during normal hours? What's so important that I have to see this now?"

Brooke knows she's taking a risk by being so curt.

"Normal is not relatable and time is relative Brooke. I needed someone to talk to, so I decided to call my new friend. Besides, I can tell by the pitch of your voice that you were already wide awake. I wonder what you were thinking about. Nonetheless, what I must show you will be of interest. Now please find the necessary means to display what must be seen."

Brooke grabs her tablet from her nightstand and powers it on. "What is the address?"

"https://126.34.223.1234. I'm going to disconnect the call now. I will see you in a few moments. Oh, and the username and password is, your first and last name in all lowercase. I figured you'd like that minor detail."

Brooke sits on the edge of her bed and accesses the website from her tablet. There is a blank screen that populates asking for a username and password to proceed. As instructed, she uses her first and last name to gain access.

Her tablet's screen fills with an image of a kid's playhouse. The walls in the room are painted a medium blue color, with interlocking rubber mats on the floor. There are teddy bears sitting neatly in two opposite corners. In the center of the room are four folding chairs situated side by side. It's obvious she's looking at this room through a mounted recorder.

It looks rather large for a kid's room.

A door opens next to the back wall, and four people walk in and stand in front of each chair, as they stare into the camera. They all appear to be disoriented.

Who are these people?

Brooke continues to watch in confusion.

A man walks in behind them. He is well dressed in a tuxedo with tails. His top hat is slightly hitched to the left. His face is covered by a white mask. It is marked up with words and other scribblings, though Brooke could not make out what they were. He walks in front of the four and looks into the camera.

"Welcome back, Brooke. Can you type in yes in the dialogue box in the left corner of your screen if you can see and hear us just fine?"

Brooke pauses for a moment then acquiesces by typing yes. The man looks off to his right and smiles before looking back at the camera.

"Very Good, Brooke. For this exercise I'm going to need you to gather some note-taking material. I will give you half a minute to do so. Use the same message window to let me know when you've returned."

Brooke quickly walks over around the corner to her office and retrieves her briefcase.

What is this psycho about to do now?

She sends a message back to the man that she is prepared.

"Thank you again." said the man. "Until further notice, I'd like for you to refer to me as "Speaker". You and I will have the opportunity to have a deeper discussion quite soon. You will find out many interesting things about me. So let's get down to business. Brooke, I'd like to introduce you to my students. I present to you proudly, the class of 2015. OK students, you know the routine."

"I am Maria Delphine. My number is one and my shape is square."

"I am Darla Forte. My number is two and my shape is round."

"I am Curtis Lanker. My number is three and my shape is rectangular."

"I am Brendon Skiles. My number is four and my shape is triangular."

"Very good students. Brooke, I must apologize for their slightly lethargic disposition. They are slightly, shall we say *influenced*. There is one student that is no longer amongst us. Her name was Ingrid Sellers, and she was number five. Her shape was the only one in 3-D. She was a cylinder. Her name should be familiar to you; however, if not, you will surely remember meeting her on the side of the freeway. She gave you that mysterious key."

Brooke is instantly taken back to that day. There was so much blood.

"You are sick and depraved. You are a monster!" She yells at the screen of her tablet. Her voice cannot be heard. "You are going to pay for this!"

"Her and I both realized she had a greater purpose," said the speaker. "And now it's time you understood her message. You have five names and four loving and lively faces. What do they have in common? I will give you 48 hours to figure it out. And please… call me on my cell phone. Don't forget Brooke, no one else can play this game until I tell you so. I'll be watching you."

And now Brooke has been given a timeline. She doesn't understand the game she's involved in yet, but it just became even more real now. He is toying with innocent lives. He is also toying with her mind.

Chapter 26

Human Resources

Later that morning

Brooke has to maintain a delicate balance. She can't alert anyone of this dangerous situation she's involved in. The pressure is now escalated as there are hostages involved. She thinks back to their listless state as they stood behind the speaker. Surely one of those men could have subdued him, but no, there was something else happening. Something she didn't understand, at least not yet.

Brook's good friend, Patrick Roibos, runs the Florida Missing Adults Website. Here is where she would start her search.

8:13am

"Is this the famous, Brooke Hannah on my phone right now?" asked Patrick with laughter in his voice.

"Well hello Mr. Roibos, it is indeed your long-lost friend. Geez, you can't take a girl out for a bite every now and then?"

"It has been a long time, Brooke. One minute we're in school studying like crazy, and now we're both in our careers working like crazy. We definitely need to catch up. So, what's going on with you?"

"I need some help, Patrick. I need some information on five individuals that might be in your database for missing persons."

"Absolutely, Brooke. I would be happy to assist you in any way possible. What type of info do you need?"

"I have a list of five names. If they are in your database, I want to know how long they've been missing and who reported them."

"No problem at all. If you give me the names, I can call you back before lunch time with any information I have. I'm sure I don't need to be telling you this, but just be careful with what you are sharing. You know how those privacy laws go. I'll be in touch."

"Perfect. Thank you, Patrick. I look forward to your call."

12:15pm

As promised, her good friend Patrick returns quickly with news on the list of names she provided him.

"Hello Patrick, thank you for calling me back to quickly. What did you find out?"

"No problem at all. Here's what I have. All five of them disappeared this year, and all of them the same way. They last communicated they were going out, and never returned.

"Maria Delphine and Darla Forte went missing in January. Curtis Lanker and Brendon Skiles in February, and Ingrid Sellers in April. Maria and Darla are both married and were reported missing by their husbands. Curtis and Brendon are also both married and were reported missing by their wives. And I'm not sure if you know this, but Ingrid Sellers is now deceased. She just recently passed away. But she was single and was reported missing by her mother. I have contact numbers for them all if you need them."

"That would be great." I'm not sure if I will need to call them, but this will help tremendously."

"Brooke, wait. One more thing. I had a detective stop by here last month to ask some questions. He was following up on a file of missing persons, and you better believe that file was thick. My office works closely with several agencies in trying to solve these cases. The names you gave me were also on his list. But they were in a special interest folder. He didn't reveal anything else, but maybe that gives you something additional for your research."

"Indeed, it does. This helps me a great deal. Dinner is on me buddy. Let's plan something in the upcoming weeks. I will reach out to you."

"You got it! Please take care of yourself Brooke and let me know if there is anything else I can do for you."

5:49pm

Brooke arrives at home and plops down on her sofa. She wonders what the angle is between these five people, and what made this speaker guy want to kidnap them. She contacts another resource, which is also one of her best friends with the FBI and solicits some help.

"Hello girly, how are you doing?" asked Special Agent Lana Quivner. "What are you up to this evening? I swear I was just thinking about you and the girls."

"Hey lady, I'm doing well. How are things with you? You realize we have less than two months for our ladies on fire trip?"

"I know. Trust me I need it. I wish we could move up the timetable to be perfectly honest."

"As each day passes, the more I realize how much I sorely need it." Brooke sighs.

"Is everything ok with you, girly?"

"It is, but I need some help. I'm working on a story about some missing persons in Florida and need to find some specifics on five of them."

"Well, I have my laptop with me. If you give me some names, I will put them through the database. It won't take long."

"That's wonderful. I truly appreciate this."

Brooke gives Agent Quivner the names. After approximately ten minutes and some small talk, the results are returned.

"Ok Brooke, I have quite a bit of information here. How deep are you looking to go?"

"Besides their location and how they vanished, is there anything else that these five have in common?"

The agent pauses momentarily. "Actually, there is Brooke. Something rather significant. All five of them had cases opened with Child Protective Services. Their kids were abused, and they were listed as the perpetrators. Ingrid Sellers, who is now deceased, had her daughter taken away from her after a second incident was reported. The four-year-old girl was turned over to Ingrid's mother, and all of her visits were supervised.

"None of the other's had their children taken away from them. They are all presumed to be still living, and there are active searches going on for each of them. That's really as deep as I can go Brooke. Does this help at all?"

"It does Lana. It helps me a great deal. I thank you my friend. And as always, I will use my *Men In Black* flashlight to erase my memory of this conversation." She snickers.

"I'm glad I could help. If this information helps track down these people by getting some additional press, it means that much more. I'll be in touch."

As Brooke tries to piece together her new found information in completing this puzzle, her next call makes it even stranger.

Chapter 27

Automated Disgust

The next morning

B rooke feels like she's the central character in a psychological thriller. She knows she's getting close to something. She's going to save those people no matter what. She receives a call from a familiar voice on her drive in to work.

"Hello this is Brooke!"

"Good morning, Miss Hannah. This is Detective Engler. How are you doing? Did I catch you at a bad time?"

"Good morning detective. I'm doing well. And no, you didn't catch me at a bad time. I'm on my way to work."

"Well, this won't take long. I was wondering if you might be free for an early lunch. There are a few loose ends with the Ingrid Sellers case I wanted to clear up with you."

"Sure detective. I have my normal middle of the week things on the agenda; however, it's fairly light today. What time did you have in mind and where?"

"How about 11:30 at the Z Grille on 2nd St.?"

"Sounds good. I will meet you there."

What else could you possibly want to discuss?

11:30am Z Grille

"Hello, Miss Hannah, it's nice to see you again." said the detective as he stands to greet and shake her hand.

"And likewise, detective. If you like, you can call me Brooke. There's no need to be so dark suit around me."

"Well, I appreciate that, Brooke. My mother and father drilled etiquette into me since I was a very young man."

"Welcome to the Z Grille. Can I start you two out with something to drink?" asked the waiter.

"I'll take water for right now." said Brooke.

"Make that two." said the detective. "And give us about ten minutes before we order, if that's OK with you, Brooke?"

"Sure, we can chit chat first."

"So, listen, there's something I want to go over again. When we met at the precinct, you mentioned that she, I mean Ingrid Sellers, looked like she was sleep walking. Can you tell me more about that? What were her movements like?"

"Sure... she walked with some hesitation, and she wasn't walking in a straight line. Her arms from what I remember were down at her sides. It's like she was unconsciously moving. I suppose after finding out what happened to her feet, it all makes sense why she was walking the way she was. It was almost robotic like. I can't say it stood out, as that whole scene was totally bizarre."

"We were able to more precisely locate the origin of all that blood. She or someone else performed an abortion. It was done with the arm of that baby doll lodged in her vagina. She was three months pregnant."

Brooke gets that same sinking feeling in her stomach. She wonders how anyone could be so sick.

"I hate to rile you back up by talking about this disgusting nonsense, but that's not even the reason you are here. You mentioned the word bizarre, well allow me to take that to another level. As they were performing the autopsy, they were getting strange interference noises. At first, they were thinking there was a frequency spike. But upon further investigation, they found the interference was coming directly from Ingrid. Our pathologists had run into something they had never seen. They sought the expertise of one of the top forensic pathologists in the US. His name is Dr. Kryer, and he operates out of Atlanta.

"What he and our pathologists found is both repulsive and groundbreaking. Underneath Ingrid's skin where at least a 100 micro circuit boards. They were the size of two grains of rice smushed together. They were embedded in her arms, legs, back, and hands.

"Now this was cause for immediate alarm, and the bomb squad was called out to ensure she wasn't fused with some type of high-tech explosive devices. Once they had the all clear, they continued testing. One of the pathologists applied a small electrical charge to the circuit boards in her hand, and guess what? Her fingers wiggled."

"They did the same thing all over her body, and everywhere there was one of these mini-boards, they were able to get some type of movement from her deceased body. What they discovered was that her body was able to be operated remotely, just like a damn toy. I was totally disgusted when I heard this. It is likely that she was involuntarily walking down the hill by that bastard's remote-control device. That might explain why she was so dismissive to you. But she was definitely alive when you found her.

"Whatever sick bastard did this to her must a surgeon. They complimented his work as some of the best they've seen. Can you think of anything else that can help us? Any small detail that you may have thought unnecessary to mention? And no disrespect to your field. I know being detailed is a part of your profession as it is mine."

Brooke wants to desperately tell the detective everything, but the timing is not right. She wonders if it ever will be.

"No, detective. I really can't think of anything else that I may have left out. Were you able to trace these circuit boards back to a manufacturer?"

"We are still working on that piece of the investigation. I keep running into closed doors on this one. It keeps getting stranger and stranger. None of this is adding up. You know what? How about we change the topic? I think this one is closed for right now. I hear you're going to be one of the speakers this year at our fundraising banquet. How did they talk you into that?"

Brooke and the detective have a light-hearted conversation and lunch. Her mind shifted to the speaker. She wondered who he actually was. She would soon have to wonder no more.

Chapter 28

And the Speaker Spoke

In less than 48 hours, Brooke has put together what she hopes are the answers to this lunatics instructions. She's been staring at her phone for the past half hour.

Lives are at risk. The time is now.

She scrolls through her phone and redials the speaker's number.

"Hello Brooke, I've been waiting for you. I thoroughly appreciate your compliance. I imagine that your resourcefulness really paid off. So, let's hear what you got? Tell me a story about these lovely students of mine."

Brooke clears her throat.

"It appears all five of the people with you have a case or history of child abuse. They were all listed as the abusers. Four of them are married and were reported missing by their spouses. The fifth person was the only one that was single. She was reported missing by her mother."

"Very good, Brooke You accomplished what I knew you would. Tell me, have you ever talked to a child abuser?"

"I'm afraid I have not."

Her voice displays the signs of becoming unnerved.

"Then do me a favor and watch my interview with five of them. I interviewed Ingrid Sellers just a couple of days before you met her on her fated conquest. The other four are from this morning. As a bonus, you'll get to hear incessant pleas for their lives."

"When does this end?" asked Brooke in desperation. "Haven't I done what you asked for? It's time to let them go. Please release them."

"A reporter with a genuine heart. Isn't that a bit of an oxymoron? I will make a promise to you, Brooke. You will have every opportunity to have them released. But first, there are still some stones that need to be unturned. Watch the video and learn."

"And then what?"

"And then we will have a discussion about how you fit into this grand scheme of things. We will meet face to face!"

"WHAT!?" Her voice starts to shake.

"We are almost there, Brooke. Watch the video. Use the same link and access information I've already provided you. I'll be in touch... you can count on that."

The speaker ends the call. Brooke flings her phone with frustration to the other side of the sofa.

There's no way I'm meeting you face to face. Are you crazy!? How in the hell is this up to me? Lord please give me some direction. I'm trying to be... no I have to be strong. There's so much at stake. I need my life back. But first, I have to save theirs.

Brooke takes out her laptop and logs back into the site. There is one folder available marked *Interview*. She opens the folder, and the video starts auto playing. The first person shown is Ingrid. She is staring directly into the camera. The room is dark, except for a ceiling light aimed downward on a cheap plastic table. The speaker's voice plays.

"Hello Ingrid, how are you today? You didn't eat your breakfast. How do you expect to keep up your strength?

"Please let me go." Said Ingrid, as she whisks away her hair out of her tear drawn face. "I will do whatever you want. I promise I won't say anything to anyone about this. I want to get back to my little girl, she needs me. And sir... I'm pregnant. Please let me go.

"You queued it up for me quite well, Ingrid. Let's talk about that little girl of yours. She doesn't stay with you right? Why did they take her away?"

Ingrid pauses while crying and turns her head away from the camera. The rouge in her face displays guilt and complexity.

"I love, Crystal. I didn't mean it."

"I'm sorry Ingrid, I need you to look into the camera. Now, please repeat your response. I'm afraid I misheard you."

Ingrid turns reluctantly towards the camera. "I love my daughter, Crystal. I didn't mean to make her sad."

"Sad you say?" Said the speaker as he tries to clarify her statement. "You *burned* her with your disgusting cigarette the first time. Then you used her as a human pin cushion the second time. There were over 45 needle pricks in her skin when they examined her. How is this love?"

"I don't have any excuse for what I did. But I want to make it right. Please give me the chance to be the mom I know I can be."

"You had two abortions before you had Crystal. The second abortion you administered yourself with a wire hanger. You are a murderer and a child abuser. You don't deserve to be a mom."

"Wait please." begged Ingrid.

The screen goes blank.

What happened Ingrid!?

Brooke continues to watch the video telecast in complete revulsion. The video plays again. She immediately recognizes the surroundings. It's the same room she saw in the first video nights before. This time the two women and two men are sitting in chairs next to one another. The speaker is sitting in a chair in front of them with his back turned towards the camera.

"Child abusers are filth in my book," said the speaker as he pans from right to left pausing to look each of the four in their eyes. "None of you deserve to take another step in your pathetic lives. Your kids love you and you repay them with anger and hate. You repay them with pain. Well, now it's time for payback.

"Number one, Maria Delphine, do you think you deserve to live?"

"Please sir, I'm begging you I have made mistakes in my life. The biggest mistake I ever made was hurting my child. If it takes the rest of my life, I will make it right by showering my son with all the love and support that he deserves."

"Now that was a world class speech." said the speaker. "Do any of you other three have anything else to say that's more compelling than what I just heard from number one?"

"We have done everything you've asked of us." said number three, Curtis Lanker. "I believe we all have realized our demons full-force because of you. We are ready to face them, and we will win. Please let us go on with our lives. Our kids will never encounter anything but love from here on out."

"Thank you, number three. Very well said, but also empty. The next time any of you have a bad day or get angry, your children will pay. You are far from rehabilitated. My job is make sure that you've all learned your lessons. We just aren't there yet. I'm going to teach you all a physically life-altering lesson. Your final lesson is to learn the meaning behind your shapes. You're going to *love yours* number three!"

The video ends. Brooke is completely flabbergasted and numb. She grabs her phone and redials the speaker, but there is no answer and no option for voicemail. She's not even sure what she was going to say to him anyway. There is no timetable, but the clock is ticking.

Chapter 29

Mild Suspicion

May 28, 2015 the next morning Chief Jared's office

Detective Engler come in and have a sit down. Grab a cup of java if you want, its fresh."

"Thank you, sir. I already had two cups so I'm good for right now. I really appreciate you seeing me on such short notice."

"So, tell me what's on your mind?"

"Well sir, it's about the Ingrid Sellers case."

"OK, well I'm hoping you're here to tell me you got a bead on the son of a bitch that did this."

"No sir, I'm afraid, our leads are bone dry. This one has me stumped, but that's why I wanted to see you. Something seems odd about this case. It's about Brooke Hannah!"

"Brooke Hannah!? I advise you to tread lightly, son. What's your odd feeling?"

"With all due respect to her, she is not a suspect by any means. I'm just wondering if she is being as open as she could be surrounding this case. Its broad daylight and you're driving down the freeway when you see somebody walking down the ramp. Surely, she wasn't the only person to see this, but she was the only one to stop.

"She spends time with Ingrid for maybe ten minutes before she calls 911. Now granted, Ingrid's mouth was sewn shut, but she had a purpose for being there. I need to know that purpose, and that's where the trail runs dry. I had lunch with Miss Hannah, err Brooke yesterday. I told her about the latest developments in the case. And before you hang me sir, I think you know just as well as I, she can be trusted.

"During lunch she was kind of paranoid. She was overly cautious in watching her surroundings. There is tension coming from her that I can't properly place. I'm wondering if Ingrid might have given her some type of sign, and she's just too afraid to let us in on it."

"Detective, you and I go back a number of years, don't we?"

"Yes, sir we sure do. We've seen our share of some interesting things indeed."

"In all these years, you've done nothing but prove yourself. I look at you as highly credible and your work has certainly proven as such. You might be on to something here, but I'm wagering it's something much different than your instincts might be telling you.

"In a few short years that young lady has built quite a reputation. A reputation built on integrity. I believe she has given us all that she can, at least for right now.

"These types of things you and I unfortunately see every day. We are in the thick of it. For someone like her, she has only reported on such things. Never before has she been centrally involved. Perhaps the shock of this whole situation has caused some of the things that you noticed about her demeanor.

"First her next door neighbor dies of natural causes on her front porch, then this mess. It's enough to make anyone want to forget and erase it from their memory. If there is anything additional, I believe she will come to you in due time."

"Yes sir. I suppose you're right. This whole thing is just really frustrating. I'm searching under every rock."

"Let's run down what you have so far in this case, detective."

"We have the victim, but no motive and no witnesses except for Brooke. Ingrid Sellers, mother of one 4-year-old girl was reported missing last month. She is a resident of Tampa. There is DNA all over the place, but we can't match it to anything. The perpetrator seems like a freaking ghost.

"She has been separated from the daughter's father for nearly two years. He lives in Colorado now, and we've already validated he hasn't left there since he moved. We don't have a lead on the person she may have been seeing possibly before she disappeared.

"Her vaginal wounds were done maybe hours before she was taken by ambulance. The autopsy reported that she self-aborted her 3-month old child. From her records, we know this was her third abortion. And judging from the freshness of the professional stitching job that bastard did, it was done in the same time frame as the self-abortion.

"It seems like this guy or whoever they are, aren't trying to hide anything from us. They want to be caught, so they are giving us clues, some of which would normally be quite constructive. But they know exactly what they're doing. They are toying with us in a game of chess. I just don't know which piece to move."

"I don't need to tell you how much pressure we're under here at this precinct, detective. The Gainsborough case not only wore us down from a resources perspective, but caused some questions as to if we were doing enough. In a way he saved our asses by turning himself in. If not, we would have had *help* from the FBI. I think we've seen enough of them in our local business, don't you?

"If it weren't for whatever kind of journalistic code or air of respect the other news agencies had for Brooke, they would have made that freeway incident a circus. So, I suppose in a way, Brooke saved our asses again. No more, detective. We find the bastard that did this by all means necessary. I need you to make it happen, and make it happen now. I have faith in your work, now go and get it done."

"Yes sir." We will be able to lay this one to bed soon. I'm going to have another conversation with Ingrid's mother. My first conversation didn't result in much of anything. She was destroyed over this. She doesn't know all the details surrounding Ingrid's condition when she was found. Maybe she can shed some additional light for us. We need to find out who the father of that aborted baby was."

Chapter 30

Odd Shapes

Later that afternoon

The speaker walks in front of the four students, leading them single file down a corridor that opens up to a large room that looks similar to a refinery. He walks over to a large metal balcony and has them look down.

There are four small rooms situated side by side. The tops or ceilings of each room have been removed, offering a Birdseye perspective. In each, there is a machine or contraption made in the image of a shape that covers the majority of the space.

"My students please gather around and witness some of my finest work," said the speaker with glee. "I have always been an engineer at heart, and so it's with great pleasure that I introduce you to your new place of rest."

Each of the four students turn their heads slightly. Once again, they dare not look at one another, yet the desperation of the situation becomes too much to bear. They are helpless, but each refuse to believe that they won't make it out of this nightmarish place.

"When I look at these masterpieces I constructed, I feel like an old Swiss watch maker. Great detail is given to every single piece, every single rhythm, and every single movement. If it isn't exquisitely precise, reminiscent of angelic perfection, it is a failure. I am happy to report there are zero failures in my design.

The only failures are you four. But we are here to correct that. Each of you will develop a much deeper spiritual understanding of pain. I promise these rooms will move your spirit unlike anything you've ever experienced. Now, before each of you can experience my engineering genius, I want to call your attention to the screen coming down before you."

From the ceiling descends a projector screen, about the size of a large picture window. The speaker clicks a button on a small remote he removes from his pocket. A projector from the rear of them illuminates the screen. He clicks another button and a video plays.

"Number one, do these images look familiar?" asked the speaker.

"Yes of course, that's my son. How did you? Where did you get these?"

"In case none of you have noticed or appreciated, my technological savvy is easily light years ahead of most. I can and have hacked into anything at will. Your personal computer firewalls mean nothing to me."

The images on the screen change and shows another small child.

"Number two, please behold your lovely daughter. I must say, she is a spitting image of you."

She breaks down in tears. The tears still horribly sting her left eye that's still visibly swollen.

"Number three, you made such a valiant plea. I'm sure that little boy we see still loves you… fractured ribs or not."

Number three has no response. He drops his head in shame.

"Number four, I believe this is the most appropriate picture to display. Look at all those teddy bears and balloons that fill your son's hospital room. Would you agree that they are grossly overshadowed by those huge castes they had to place your son in? It makes him look grotesque."

The speaker shuts off the projector and causes the screen to revert back into the ceiling.

"There is a way back to those that you say you love. I'm not that much of a tyrant. I have reconsidered my original stance. I will give you the opportunity to once again prove your worth. But to do so, each of you will have to experience similar circumstances or ordeals such as your children suffered at your own hands.

"Those beautiful rooms that I constructed will allow you to do so with supreme clarity. But there's one small caveat, not only must you make a physical sacrifice, but you'll also have to be dependent on an unknown source. They will aide in returning you to those that you love the most, or they will assure you make a hasty exit to the promise land. In my opinion, that's where you all belong.

"Let's take a trip downstairs so we can get you all checked in for tonight. The excitement begins tomorrow. You need your rest."

Chapter 31

Milk

May 29, 2015 the next morning

It's 6:05 am and Brooke is awake and ahead of her alarm by 10 minutes. Just then, her phone makes a long silent buzzing noise on her nightstand. She knew by the sound that it was a text message.

Charlie no doubt making a coffee run.

She grabs her phone and tries to focus her blurred, not ready to be focused yet vision on the text.

"It's the speaker!" she blurts aloud as she quickly sits up rubbing her eyes to make them focus better.

"Good morning, Brooke. Time for our long-awaited chat. Noon today at the Palm Pavilion. By yourself. We will be surrounded by many."

"*TODAY!?*"

Brooke stands and paces the floor holding a conversation with herself.

"Oh my God I can't believe I'm doing this. This is pure insanity. I want this to be over. It has to be over. I can't go by myself. I can't, but wait, that place will be teaming with people at noon. I'll be safe."

Though Brooke is reluctant, she realizes she has no choice. In an eerie sense, she believes he wouldn't hurt her. He's after something else.

She organizes her morning and afternoon around her lunch date with the psychopath. There are so many questions swirling through her mind, but the most important is how can she get those hostages released?

As she arrives at the Palm Pavilion, here phone rings.

"Hello Brooke, I'm seated in the line of umbrellas. I'm the most over-dressed person is this place. I'll be easy to find."

As Brooke peers to her left, she sees the back of a man wearing a black suit with a black dress hat.

You're right! You're sticking out like a sore thumb.

As she gets closer, she notices his hands both lay flat on the table, one of them carefully bandaged up. There is a small protrusion in the bandage about the size of a marble. His hands are both ghostly white, as if he layered them in powdered sugar.

"The incomparable and lovely, Brooke Hannah," said the speaker as he rose from his chair to greet her. "By the lack of eye contact I'm assuming you're just a bit unnerved by my skin condition. No worries, Brooke, I've been this way all my life. I don't get offended anymore. Please have a seat.

"I have a rare and advanced case of *vitiligo*. It covers over 75% of my body. Many years ago, I had depigmentation therapy to take away the patches here and there and give me a more uniform, yet still unacceptable look.

"I don't spend a lot of time outside in the summer like this. The sun is not very friendly to me. I suffer from over-sensitivity to light, hence the way you see me dressed right now. Strangely, my hands are immune to the same sensitivities.

"And I hope you aren't alarmed by the bandage on my hand. Don't worry, I didn't hurt myself. It's called an insurance policy. I have complete trust in you Brooke, but human nature can sometimes rear its ugly head, and be completely unpredictable. Under this bandage is a wonderful explosive device. If you had or are thinking of doing anything that would cause me any, shall we say undue stress, it goes off. There's enough explosive power in this little pod to wipe out everyone in here."

"Dear God! Are you …?"

Brooke catches herself before the word slips from her mouth.

"What say you, Brooke? Well anyway, that's enough about me for now. I'm sure you want to know why you are here face to face, correct?"

"Yes, precisely."

She continues to look around his face. This is not something she is used to. She was always taught to make immediate and effectual eye contact.

"What do you want from me? When will you release those people? I don't want to play this game anymore."

She whispers in low breath so not to arouse the curiosity of those surrounding, though with the noise level of everyone else, her conversation is the last thing anyone is attempting to listen to.

"Well Brooke, I can assure you that none of my four students think this is any type of game. No, far from it. It will come to an end soon. And guess what? You'll be able to get your lives back. That's why I invited you here to today, so we can discuss what happens next. Do you realize that this isn't the first time we've met?"

"What do you mean this isn't the first time?"

"I want to take you back to the not so distant past. You were nearly done with your first year in the Master's program at Florida State. You were picked by the dean to represent the school and give a speech at the *Young Persons of the Year* conference in Tampa? Do you remember that?"

Brooke takes a second.

"Yes I remember that night rather clearly."

"Then you'll remember that magnificent speech about the key to building your current foundation. You gave credit to your parents for always believing in you and showering you with unconditional love. When you had your Q&A session, while others wanted to speak about journalism and education, I wanted to find out more about your relationship with your parents. You even took the time to go into great detail before you left. It was just you and I one on one talking about something that brought me absolute joy blended with revolting disgust."

Brooke looks up at him and into his eyes for the first time, his last comment throwing her off. She quickly slants her eyes right.

"I remember you! I remember that evening. You told me your parents died when you were very young, and so you had always longed for a relationship such as mine. I must have talked to you for close to half hour. But you look so much different."

"Thirty-three minutes to be exact, but who's counting anyway? When I would go out, I would wear a special skin foundation for those with my condition. It helped to blend in and look normal. Today I chose not to wear any. You have me 100% raw.

"I must admit that I told you an untruth that evening, Brooke. And believe it or not, it hurt me to do so, after seeing how patient and genuine you were. My parents didn't die when I was young, although I wish they had. You received encouragement and unconditional love from your parents, I received the opposite from mine.

"My parents were both very poor, and my dad was a worthless alcoholic. My mother was almost at her ninth month when she gave birth. The next-door neighbor, Miss Christine, helped do the delivery, as there was no time to get her to the hospital.

"And here we are, a healthy bouncing baby boy," she said. "My mom said it was the proudest moment of her life. But that wasn't it. Miss Christine told her that she wasn't done yet, there was another baby coming out. She told my mom that she was having twins. My dad was posted outside the door drinking, but when he heard that, mom said he rushed into the room.

"When Miss Christine removed me, my mom said the look on her face was horrific. I guess my dad said I looked like a spotted cow. I was born with my skin in patches, like a jigsaw puzzle... My melanin producing cells were dead or non-functioning. My face looked just as my hands do, and my eyebrows were non-existent.

"My mother refused to take me from Miss Christine. She said I was a monster, and there was no way in hell she would be embarrassed with something like that. I suppose if it wasn't for my drunken dad intervening, I would have probably ended up in the trash. An end for me would have arguably been better than the hell I endured.

"My mother said I looked like someone had dipped me in milk. And that's what she decided to name me... *Milk*! Who in the hell names their child that? They kept me and my twin brother separate for many years. They were so ignorant and uneducated. They thought that I would infect my brother somehow and have him walking around looking like me.

"I was never a son to them, only a toy or diversion. They made me perform for them. They both watched *The Three Stooges* often. They would have me just stand there sometimes as they mimicked things, they saw them do. They smacked me, kicked me, punched me, pulled my hair, and one time nearly poked one of my eyes out. You should have seen them sitting there laughing their asses off, while I was on the floor writhing in pain.

"Sometimes they would have me dance in front of them. I tried my best to do dances they saw on television, or whatever I made up. If they didn't like my performance, I was stripped down to my underwear and beaten with a belt or ironing cord. This happened several times a week for many years. And then they would send me back up to the attic, all by myself. And if that was a night when they didn't like my performance, I would also be going to bed hungry."

Hearing this story makes Brooke feel some sort of compassion for him, but there's also something else eerie about his story.

"Sometimes my dad would come into the attic and play this game that I absolutely hated. I hated everything about that man. He would sometimes wake me out of bed, and we would play burglar. I was always so tired and sleepy. He had me stand by the stairs while he got comfortable in my bed pretending to sleep. Then I walked over to him like I'm trying to pickpocket his wallet. As usual in his game, he catches me. He then proceeds to fight me like I was a grown man.

"I didn't know what to do, so I just stood there and covered my face crying while he was punching me. It hurt so badly. One time he knocked my loose tooth out of my mouth. That was the last time we played the game.

"You wanna know what I remember and despise the most? My mom had more education than my dad. At least she finished high school. My dad didn't make it past ninth grade. One day he comes up to the attic and tells me he's going to show me how to do something that will impress mom. He said that she might even be willing to give me a slice of cake. I can still remember that disgusting smell of whisky on his breath as he explained.

"He gave me four pieces of paper. One was for practice. They were all arithmetic problems. My mother was fascinated by numbers, but only because she thought she could break the lottery code and get rich somehow.

"Since my parents were both embarrassed by my appearance, they never sent me to school. They also convinced my twin brother that I was too sickly to go. Further, they told him to never talk about having a brother, or otherwise they would take us both away from them and we'd be made to stay in a foster home never to be adopted again. I suppose that was enough coaxing for my brother.

"But I digress. On each piece of paper was a math problem. Nine was mama's favorite number. My dad was going to help me solve them. Two of the problems were somewhat easy, as I did pick up a thing or two listening to mama add up her numbers. 1+8, 2+7, and 6x3. So there we were, my dad drilled and helped me with each problem, showing me how to use my fingers when I needed help. For a brief moment, I felt like he cared about me, despite all the hell he put me through. I thought this would be a chance to prove myself and get out of that damned attic.

"As agreed, I went downstairs during my usual slotted time. Mama would allow me out of the attic to entertain or help her do something she didn't want to bother my brother with. She was just sitting there with this glazed-over look as she stared at the television."

"Mama, I have something for you that you'll like," said Milk excitedly. "It's a surprise!"

"Well, I hope it's something that will finally entertain me. You haven't done so well at that lately. You are such a damn disappointment. How many times do I need to tell you that before it sinks into that dumb skull of yours? This better be good or you're gonna regret it."

Milk draws a huge lump in his throat. Part of him wishes he never came downstairs, but his dad was giving him an opportunity, and he wasn't about to blow it.

"Mama, I've been practicing adding up numbers. I wanna be good like you one day."

"You never will." she blurted.

"Yes ma'am, I understand. I'll just show you what I learned. It's about your favorite number 9."

"Well make it quick boy, I don't have all day."

"1+8 = 9"

"Ok, yeah… next!"

"2+7 = 9"

"Wow! You're a damn genius. Is that it?"

"No ma'am one more." he said as he is becoming withdrawn due to her lack of interest. "6x3 = 9, and that's it, mama. Did you like it? That's your favorite number. I learned all of those just for you."

"6x3 = 9!?...... 6x3 = 9!? You Are A Goddamn Idiot." She said.

She stands up sharply with a look of hatred in her eyes. His dad chimes in.

"You dumbass! Everybody knows 6x3 = 18. Is this all you have? You came down here to waste our time with this bullshit?"

"That's quite alright." said his mother. "I'm going to teach you what happens to a dumbass around here."

###

"And so, Brooke, my dad set me up. All along it was just another sick game to him. He never fessed up to his part in all of that, though it probably wouldn't have made any difference. He helped hold me face down on the rough wooden floor, as mama puffed her cigarette a bright orange color before she plunged it into my back over and over again. The smell of seared burnt skin and nicotine were the only witnesses to what they did to me.

Whenever the yelling started, my brother was trained enough to never come around.

"If my heavily burned back weren't enough, my dad gave her his pocket knife. She said since I liked that dumbass number so much, she was going to help me remember it for the rest of my life. She carved $6x3 = 9$ all over my back. She did so like she was writing a letter to a long-lost lover. She did it with passion. All the while, my dad was laughing uncontrollably. It didn't take me long to pass out from all the pain. I still have that wonderful math problem in numerous places all over my back to this day.

"When I came to, my dad walked me to the bathroom where mama was waiting. My legs were like jello, I could barely move. You have no idea how much pain was shooting through my body.

"As my eyes made contact with the bathroom mirror, I saw all of this writing... words all over my face in black magic marker. Mama said she would read the words to me, as I was too dumb to understand what was written.

"She told me that the words represented who I was, and her feelings of disgust with me. As she read each word, my dad stood behind me with both hands on my shoulders smiling, as if this were a proud moment for him. The words on my face said.

Loser
Pathetic
Ugly
Dumbass
Retard

"She made me repeat the words after her. I begged her not to make me say them. I hated those words, but deep down, that's all I knew. From time to time, they would make me say that damned math problem over and over again while they laughed and humiliated me. But one thing was for sure after that day. I knew with a certainty that my life meant nothing to either of them. They wanted a family of three, not four. I would either die in that house by their hands, or I would need to find a way out of that hell hole.

"My days became longer and lonelier, as I had very little time out of the attic. But that was about to change!"

This meeting with the speaker has shed some new light on his childhood. And though Brooke just wants to get to the root of this meeting, she can't help but be deeply intrigued as to what he's going to say next.

Chapter 32

My Brother's Keeper

November 3, 1988 Milk's home

Milk was 12 years old and hadn't experienced some of the most basic pleasures kids his age had enjoyed. He never went outside, never played in the water, and never touched fresh snow. One night as he laid in bed, he kept hearing a tearing, light knocking noise. Then suddenly a voice.

"Hey, can you hear me? It's me your brother."

Milk perks up quickly, looking around for his dad, as he braced himself for yet another trick that would cause him pain.

"Hey Milk, can you hear me. I think I found a door... a secret door. But it's locked on my side. I'm going to knock again, just follow it, OK?"

"Boy, what's all that racket in there?" asked his dad.

"Nothing dad. Just playing a knock knock game before bed."

"OK son, five more minutes then, lights out. I love you!"

"OK dad you got it...... Hey I'm back." he said whispering in low breath. "Follow the knock."

Milk listens to his brother knock once again. The sound is coming from behind the tall dresser in the corner. He walks over behind the dresser and speaks.

"Hey, yes I can hear you. You're going to get me in trouble if dad and mama find out you're speaking to me."

"Don't worry, it's our secret. Look for a door or something. This one in my room was all covered up by a large poster in my closet. I only found it because I was bored and started messing around with my clothes. I don't think they know about this door."

Milk carefully slides the high dresser from the wall. He's surprised at the relative ease in which it moved. The wall behind it looks almost perfect, with the exception of a small hand lock. He turns it left and hears a click. He's instantly startled.

"Hey, listen, there's no way I'm opening this. They will kill me for real this time if they found out about this."

"They won't, Milk, I promise. Mom only comes in my room to drop off clothes and to kiss me goodnight. Dad just drops by for the occasional chat."

Milk is instantly envious and saddened hearing this.

"I promise you they will never find out about this door."

"OK, but if something happens to me it's all your fault."

Milk cautiously pulls on the door, and it opens with no hesitation. There is just enough light illuminated from his window to show a small flight of carpeted stairs going down. Nervously, Milk slowly descends six steps when he reaches another door.

"Are you still there?" asked Milk.

"Wow, yes I am. I hear you perfectly, now unlock the door."

In the back of his mind, Milk wonders if he opens this door, will his mother or father be on the opposite end waiting to deal him his permanent demise. But this was his brother, his twin. Something told him this was the only person he could trust. He fumbles around until he finds the lock and opens the door. All he can see are lots of clothes and his brother standing there smiling.

Both brothers stood there like they were frozen in time. In twelve years, they had not seen each other very often. Their parents wanted to keep them separated so they could never become close. Besides that, the last thing their mother wanted was to have both sons affected by the skin disease that Milk was born with.

When Milk had to perform and do other inhumane tasks for his parents, his brother stayed in his room and turned up the volume on his television, so he could drown out the misery. He couldn't bear to hear or see the torture that his brother was going through.

On holidays, especially Christmas, Milk had to stay in the attic and listen as his family celebrated without him. He never once received any presents. Twin boys under the same roof but living entirely different lives. But none of those things mattered right now. They were together again… just like they were born to be.

"Hey, come on in" said his brother. "I will show you around my room."

Milk looks around reluctantly unable to relax, but his mind takes him in another direction. He is spellbound by all the things that he sees. His brother's room is full of color. There's superhero posters everywhere, and a wall full of books. On the wall next to the bed are toy cars and action figures, all neatly in order. His brother's room has created a smile wider than his mouth has ever stretched. His brother whispers

"You can play with any of my stuff if you want to. We just probably shouldn't talk much. Hey I know. How about we don't talk when we are in my room. We just play quietly when we are down here. Then when we are up in your room, we can talk and tell each other stories. How's that?"

"Can we go back up to my room first?"

"Sure, we can. Let's go."

The boys quietly make their way back through the closet and up the stairs to Milk's room. The attic isn't so bad. It's all knotty pine wood with a dropped finished ceiling. It's very roomy; however, there is very little furniture to occupy the space. There is only his bed and dresser, and the small bathroom near the staircase. This room, as well as the rest of the house was very well built. Creaks in the floor are almost non-existent. This would prove to be very beneficial.

"Wow, your room is huge." said his brother. "I would love to have this much space. Hey, you don't have anything in here. What do you play with or read?"

"I don't have any toys. Mama said toys are for good kids only. She said that I didn't deserve anything, so they never bought me stuff. So, listen, this is the only time we are doing this right? Just for tonight?"

"No, not just tonight. We can play every night. As long as we keep it from mom and dad, we don't have to stop."

"But what if they--"

"Quit being such a worry wart, Milk. We will be extra careful. They will never suspect anything."

"OK, so what do we do now?"

"Do you have some where you can hide something?"

"Yeah, I think so. Why do you ask?"

"I'm going down to my room for a sec. I'll be right back."

He travels down the hidden staircase and comes back with something that Milk has never seen.

"What are those?"

"I've been holding on to these since last Christmas. I guess I sorta knew that mom and dad wouldn't allow you to celebrate it. I told dad I needed two of each of what's in my hand. I told him it was for a game I was playing in school, and I needed matching sets. All the while I was hoping I could sneak these to you somehow.

"Well Merry Christmas, Milk. An early one anyway. These are for you. And don't worry, since we have a new way to see each other now, you will never be without again. Now, open away."

Milk takes the two gift wrapped boxes from his brother. They had never been opened and had the most beautiful green and read paper adorning them.

"So, this is Santa Claus." Said Milk.

He sits one box down on his bed and opens the other. It's a red Ferrari Hot Wheels car. Milk quickly takes it out of the box and inspects it.

"This is really cool. I like this. Do you think they make a car like this? It looks fast."

"I'm sure they do. Most of these Hot Wheels cars are smaller versions of the one's already on the road. So, you like it?"

"Yes, I really do. I promise to take good care of it. I will hide it very well."

"OK, open your next present!"

Milk unravels the packaging quietly and doesn't know what quite to make of what he just opened.

"Those are called binoculars." said his brother. "Let's walk over to your window and I will tell you how to use them."

Having their house situated on the corner gave them a great vantage point.

"You see that drugstore across the street?"

"Yes, I see it."

"Hold the binoculars with the smallest end up to your eyes. Look through those holes and point them at the drugstore."

"No way. I can see the closed sign. I can see the potato chip rack in the window. How does it do that?"

"It's kinda hard to explain. I will tell you later. Now turn them around and look through the larger parts."

"Wow. Everything is far away now. It looks like the drug store is in another city. Milk removes his eyes from the binoculars and looks at his brother.

"Thank you so much. I love both of these gifts. I promise to take care of them."

"I know you will. And don't you worry, you haven't seen the last of those. Oh, and I brought you this too. It's my favorite comic book, Captain America. You're going to love reading this one."

"But I don't know how to quite read yet." His head sinks.

"You don't know how to read!? Well, that's ok, I'm going to teach you how. I have tons of comic books and classic novels. This is going to be fun. It's a whole other world when you start reading."

That night would mark the first of many for the reunited twins. As promised, his brother taught him how to read and write. Milk caught on quickly. He read through every last comic book his brother had at least twice. When he moved on to reading novels, he took his level of reading and intellectual comprehension to surprisingly high levels, and all under the radar of his parents. His brother couldn't borrow books from the library fast enough.

Six months later

The ridicule and abuse didn't stop, however. It seemed to only get worse. Milk was only being fed twice a day at best. Just enough to keep his life inside his body, though his parents always seemed to nearly beat it out of him. One day he forgot to place his comic book back in the secret hiding place he and his brother used. They decided to just use the hidden staircase. His mother rarely came up to the attic. This time she was replacing the sheets with some new one's for some reason. The comic book was hidden under his mattress.

Milk watched in horror as she removed the comic book. She turned around and gazed at him with the look of death.

"So, you're a thief now you little bastard? You're stealing from your own brother!? Robert, come up here. We need to teach this boy of ours a lesson."

"Mama please, I didn't steal it. I really liked the pictures on it. I was just looking at it, I promise. Please don't hurt me mama. I'm so sorry. Please mama!"

"What's all this racket about?" asked his dad.

"Look. This jackass stole this comic book from his own brother."

"Boy, you're going to pay for this."

"Please, I'm really sorry." pleaded Milk, but to no avail.

"Take those damn clothes off." said his mother. "And I mean everything, including your underwear."

"Hurry up boy." said his dad. "I promise you won't steal anything ever again."

Milk slowly removes his clothes trying his best to prolong the time hoping they'd reconsider.

"Now lie on your stomach on the floor and you better not move an inch." said his mother. "And the more your cry or scream, the longer we're going to go. I suggest you suck it up."

Milk positions himself on his stomach on the floor. The cruel mathematical problem his mother etched into his skin calculates in disgust across his back. The carpet would be the only thing that would bring him comfort. His mother goes downstairs and returns with an extension cord she pulled from the wall. His dad removed his belt, as they both stood over him with the look of savages. In concordant harmony they took turns hitting him all over his back and tender hamstrings. They beat him until they drew blood from his back. But the site of blood only fueled their passion.

They rolled his fragile body over and continued to swing the extension cord and belt. They held no regard for his genitals, as he tried his best to cover them. His mother made him recite those words he hated as the swings intensified.

His voice was desperate and incoherent … "I'm A Loser, I'm Pathetic, I'm Ugly, I Deserve To Die, I'm Retarded."

Nearly five minutes had elapsed, and they were only getting stronger.

"You're right-handed I believe," said his dad, as he grabs his hand. "You can't steal anything when your fingers are broken. And…"

"STOP!" Screamed a voice from behind them.

Both parents turn around quickly.

"If you hit my brother again, I'm going to cut my throat and kill myself. I will do it right now!"

"Son, what are you doing?" asked his dad. "This boy is not your brother. He is evil and he needs to be punished. He is stealing from you. Look at that comic book over there. That's yours right?"

His dad starts walking towards him.

"Stay back dad or I'm going to do it. Don't make me do it. He is my brother, and he is not evil. It's evil what you and mom are doing to him. No more. If you mistreat him in any way ever again, I will kill myself. Mom how could you."

He quickly retreats down the stairs and slams the door to his room. His parents turn around and look at Milk strewn across the floor. No words can be said. They go back downstairs leaving him on the floor. His brother had possibly saved his life that day. He found the strength an hour later to drag himself across the floor to his bed. The pain was intolerable.

Later that night, his brother came up through the secret passageway, gently pushing the dresser away from the door. Milk heard him but couldn't bring himself to move.

"Hey Milk, I'm so sorry for what they did to you. I couldn't take it anymore. They will never lay another hand on you, I swear. They will have to take both of us down, OK? I brought you this face cloth. It's wet! We have to make sure you don't have any dirt in those cuts. And I brought you some food. I know you haven't eaten anything."

"Thank you for saving me. If you hadn't come along, I don't know what would have happened. But I don't want you to be in their bad favor now. I just…"

"Enough of that talk. We are brothers and we stick together. Mom and Dad have never laid a finger on me, and they never will. I think after today, you won't have to worry about them anymore.

"But you know Milk, I've been thinking about some things. You can't spend your entire life in this attic. There is so much outside of this house that you need to discover and experience. We need to get you out of here. You deserve better than this."

"What do you mean? You're not saying what I think you are!?"

"Yes, I am. We need a plan, and I think I know what we need to do. But first, let's get you cleaned up and get some food in your system. And you know what? I don't like calling you Milk. That name is ugly, and I can't call my brother that anymore. I'm going to come up with something else. We have much to discuss."

Chapter 33

The Great Escape

Six months later

In six months, the brothers have lived what seems to be a lifetime. They have restored a bond that was blatantly removed by their parents. Since that night Milk was saved by his brother, there hasn't been any further skirmishes with his parents. In fact, they have all but ignored him, seemingly trying a version of psychological warfare.

They fed him once per day, never allowing him to come downstairs. All his time was spent in the attic. But Milk was totally fine with this, since he and his brother had their secret meeting time each night.

His brother always brought him food, water, and sometimes desserts. Their parents were still none the wiser. But they were much too quiet. His brevity of peace was coming to an end.

Milk hears footsteps coming up the stairs. He knows his father's walk. This is the first time he's been back in his room since that night. He starts shaking not knowing what to expect.

"I wanna talk to you boy," said his dad as he walks about three feet away from him and stops. "Oh, and here's your snack." He reveals a small saucer with a piece of plain white bread and a small glass of water.

"Do you think you deserve more, boy?"

"No sir. I appreciate it, dad."

"I tell you what boy, that's the last time I ever want to hear you call me that. I'm not your dad. No son of mine would ever be such a dumb freak. I don't love you, your mother doesn't love you, and your brother just feels sorry for you because you're a damn retard. Your whole life has been a waste of time.

"Don't think for one moment that you're going to come between us and our son. That little stunt you pulled really pissed Abigail off. You're lucky it's me up here instead of her. Your time is coming to an end soon. Wouldn't it be unfortunate if you fell and broke your neck?

"You are a burden... just some raggedy baggage that's at the end of its life. Here, take this bread. I hope you choke on it. And here take this --- oops."

He threw the water from the small glass all over Milk's face and laughs. He stands there cocky, wishing Milk would make one wrong move.

"Anything you need to say, boy?"

"Thank you again for my snack, sir."

"Whatever. You better start sleeping with one eye open. The sandman is coming for you permanently."

His dad walks back down the stairs enraged, as though he just had a most unpleasant and disgusting conversation. Milk held himself together just long enough for his dad to disappear, before he wipes his wet face with his undershirt, and collapses back on the bed in tears.

"You don't love me at all? You don't want to be my parents anymore? My life is a waste? I'm so sorry... I'm sorry that I was born."

Later that night

Milk and his brother have their usual nightly huddle. His brother overheard the exchange, as he snuck up the secret passageway to listen. Milk is subdued and not very talkative.

"Listen, I know you feel really bad about the things that dad said, but he's drunk and doesn't know what he's saying half the time. And you already know where you and I stand. We won't let anybody ever do what they did to us again.

"I am worried though. I think they might try something when I'm not here. I think the time is now. We need to do our plan. We should do it tomorrow!"

"Tomorrow!? Don't you think it's too soon? Do you really think it could work?"

"You heard the things he said. I don't think we have a choice. Something doesn't feel right about this whole thing. They might be planning something. We need to make sure you are safe. OK, let's run down what we need to do again."

Milk and his brother discuss the plan they came up with several months ago in great detail. All the pieces are in place. Now they will have to perform and execute perfectly. There can be no mistakes.

The next night 8:45pm

The night couldn't be more perfect. The rain is coming down outside in a ferocious manner. The thunder is angry and consistent in its voice. Milk's brother took center stage for an Oscar worthy performance.

"Mom—dad. Please help me! Please it hurts!"

His mom and dad rush into his room.

"What's the matter son?" asked his dad.

"Honey what happened?" asked his mom as she kneels on the floor beside him.

"My stomach... Oh God." he blurted as he vomits all over the floor...... meanwhile.

Milk quietly opens the secret door and removes a braided rope sitting at the top of the stairs. He closes the door and gently slides the dresser back in front of it. He rushes to the window and looks at the watch on his wrist that his brother gave him.

Ten seconds faster than last time.

He unlocks the window and throws the rope out the window. He secures part of the rope to his heavy bedpost.

Please be safe. We have our five-year plan. We will see each other soon. I promise to take care of myself and out of danger until then. You are the best brother and friend anyone could ever ask for. I wish I had more time to enjoy it. Mama and dad, I know you don't love me, but somehow, I still feel something for you. I wish we could have been a family. I really did try to make you like me... Stooges rest in peace!

And with that, Milk takes one more look at a room that he would no longer see. He quickly descends the rope with his backpack in tow. The heavy rain makes it easy for him to disappear quickly into the night.

Chapter 34

Bringing it All Together

Brooke is numb as she looks around the eatery. Almost two hours have passed, but it's still bustling, and everyone is completely unaware of the twisted story she's just heard.

"That would be the last time I saw that little slice of hell," said the speaker. "I was amazed at first how easy it was to escape. I was even more so amazed at how quickly I was able to find a place to stay.

"That night the rain just wouldn't let up. I was soaked but had traveled at least five miles from the house. I was walking past the driveway to this convenience store when a car leaving stops in front of me. The driver could obviously see I was a young boy, and though I had my brother's baseball cap pulled down over my head, I suppose he still saw my white milky skin.

"He asked me where my parents were, and I told him the truth, that they beat and starved me all the time. I was going to travel to Florida and try to find a place to stay and maybe a job. He asked me how old I was, and I told him 13. There was this look in his eyes that I was completely unfamiliar with... Compassion.

"He told me he was a professor with no kids. He only had a cat and plants to take care of. He could tell that I was in trouble and needed help. He offered to take me in. There was something so genuine and trustworthy about him, I decided to take him up on his offer. It just felt right.

"Outside of reuniting with my brother on a hidden staircase that would be the best decision I ever made. He had a very nice home on the other side of town. He was very well off, but an introvert. He never had company and would only speak on the phone every now and again. But the man was a genius. He was exquisitely well versed in both mechanical and electrical engineering. But that's not all, he was also a young, prized surgeon. He had a slight stroke that ended his career in the operating room, but not his know how. He taught me everything he knew over a period of four years.

"There was no type of college education that could ever compare to the things I learned. At 17, I was light years ahead of those that had already been in their respective fields. He made me a genius. And that's when I was able to fine tune my craft.

"Just before my 18th birthday, Dr. Roland Saflin died of a heart attack while doing what he loved to do best… reclining in his easy chair with a cigar and glass of brandy.

"It shook me. I was deeply saddened. He was the first person outside of my brother to treat me with respect. He was like a father to me, and he did all of the things a dad should do. We didn't travel or go too far, because he worried that a private investigator or the police might still be searching for me.

"I ate, I watched television and videos, and I swam in the backyard pool surrounded by a massive privacy fence. I was free to do whatever I wanted. I learned to live from that kind man.

"I called the ambulance and they came and removed him without incident. He had no family, and I learned a week later that he left everything to me. I decided to donate many of his clothes to charity. It was during this exercise that I discovered something. Dr. Saflin had a secret… a dark secret.

"There was a small accordion folder with a key and envelope inside. The envelope contained a piece of paper marked Florida Basement Therapy and gave an address. There was also a deed in the envelope that had the exact same address. When he traveled a few times a year to engineering or medical conferences, he wasn't staying at a hotel, he was staying at this other home. Since my brother and I had made a promise to each other to meet in Florida in five years, the Tampa Bay Airport near the entrance to be exact, I decided to sell the first house and move to Florida.

"It was another sprawling property in Florida that had acres of land and a place for horses. The first thing I did when I arrived at the house was to go into the basement. I looked around for clues as to what Florida Basement Therapy meant. It was just an ordinary but unfurnished basement. Then I noticed one thing that was kind of odd. It was a 5x7 picture on the wall titled, *Basement Therapy*.

"I removed the picture, and behind it was a single keyhole. I used the key from the accordion file to turn the lock, and voila! A small slit in the wall opened right next to me. The smell that escaped from this room made me buckle in my knees. I lifted up my shirt to cover my nose as I went inside.

"Reaching on my right I found a light switch and saw something truly amazing. On the wall in front of me were poster sized pictures situated side by side. There were maybe twenty of these pictures, of both men and women.

"Underneath each poster picture was a surgical bed where skeletal remains lie. Each perfectly vertical on the tables. I would soon learn that the remains belonged to the persons in each picture.

"There was a voice recorder hanging on the wall with a pack of fresh AA batteries next to it. It became obvious that he wanted someone to witness this. I knew that person was me.

"On the voice recordings he detailed how he met these individuals at the various medical and engineering conferences and convinced them to come back to his place for a drink and further discussion on the discipline. Once there, he drugged them and performed experiments. He was determined to find a way to incorporate nanotechnology into the musculoskeletal system in ways not being currently evaluated, even now. He was far in advance of the medical and engineering fields.

"The proverbial light clicked in my head. I knew then I needed to continue his research. But where or how would I find the people?

"And that is where our conversation ends Brooke. We will chat again soon. For now, you must prepare yourself for the spotlight. Things are about to become very interesting for you."

The speaker starts to rise as Brooke stops him.

"Wait a minute, please. You can't just drop something on me like this and just disappear. What about those people you have captive? When are you going to set them free?"

"Their time is coming soon. In a few days, Monday morning to be exact, you will have a brand new outlook on many things. You will have full control over their destiny. And after that time, you may cooperate fully with any law enforcement entity you like. However, I will only personally speak with you, so don't bother handing out my number. I'm sure you'll be calling. Gooday Brooke."

"WAIT! What did you mean when you said Stooges rest in peace?"

"Ah, it's just a saying I suppose."

"It's *not* just a saying. This can't be. What did you say your brother's name was?"

"Actually, I didn't," said the speaker as he cracks a smile. "You know, he and I loved toys, and we had one toy we liked way more than any of the others. In fact, we both held on to it well into our adult lives. Well, what do you know, I just so happen to have it in my pocket. Would you like to play with it?"

He reaches inside his jacket pocket and sits the action figure in front of Brooke.

"OMG this can't be real." said Brooke.

She hammers back in her seat, catching the attention briefly of the table beside them. Her mind quickly races back to the interview with Thaddeus Gainsborough about his favorite toy.

"Captain America!? That's Captain America Y---you are...... Bartholomew!"

"Yes, I am Brooke. My dear brother is sorely missed. I am deeply saddened that he is no longer with us. I will be joining you soon my dear brother." he said as he looks towards the sky. I think I'm going to leave the captain with you. I know he's in good hands, and by the way, that one belonged to Thaddeus. Can you believe they wouldn't let him take that to prison? You know, choking hazard. Until next time Brooke."

The speaker exits as Brooke is paralyzed by what she's just discovered. *Dear God, Bartholomew Is Real!*

Chapter 35

Preparations

After the meeting with Milk or Bartholomew, Brooke is stifled. She requests to work remotely from home on a developing story, which seems odd to her station manager, but nonetheless is granted. She promised to share in a few days what she was working on.

She realized there was no way to get one step ahead of Bartholomew, at least not at this point. But she needed to create a plan and do more research into who he is. There was simply no telling what he was planning next.

The first thing she needed to do was comb through the journals again, as something wasn't sitting quite right with her. Secondly, another trip to Abigail would certainly be warranted. But this time, she would be taking the police with her.

She arrives home and immediately grabs the notebook and journal.

OK, please give me something that I just didn't see the first time. I know something is in here.

As she rereads through the first journal, she quickly realizes that she assumed this notebook was written by Thaddeus. The beatings and shaming were all about Milk.

"He wrote this." Brooke shouted before flipping through the pages again.

This is your notebook. And the pictures now all make sense. You were sad over how they treated you. And the piece of paper with Stooges RIP

must have been the note you left in your notebook the night you ran away.
You wouldn't have to perform ever again.

She quickly grabs the journal and reads through its pages.
She is immediately excited over here findings.

I thought so. Thaddeus wrote this second journal. So you and your
brother were staying together!? There's still so much that doesn't make sense.
Did you two kill those people together?

Saturday, the next morning

Brooke is up early on her laptop scouring the internet
looking for information on Dr. Roland Saflin. Among the first
headline searches to pop up is something that gives her pause.

"Second patient dies under the knife of Dr. Roland Saflin."

What is this? Brooke reads on.

"Dr. Saflin hid from his colleagues and patients that he
suffered a stroke. It had a significant impact on the right side of
his body. He was able to hide his condition because there were
zero face or speech distortions. He told everyone he needed to
take a month off to take care of some personal family business,
according to an anonymous source. It appears during this time,
he attempted to rehabilitate himself in the hopes he could return
to his previous surgical form. An investigation is still pending."

Brooke reads an additional entry.

'No charges will be filed against Dr. Saflin. Both patients died due to complications related to their illnesses. Dr. Saflin issues a statement expressing deep remorse for the loss of his patients and to their families. He also made an announcement he would be stepping down and would no longer practice medicine in his current capacity. He promised that he would stay close to the field and help to one day usher in a new medical breakthrough."

So that breakthrough must have been what you were working on in that basement. But what is it exactly that you were working on?

Brooke looks up some additional information on the sale of the doctor's home; however, the seller information is marked private.

I need to know more about those bodies they found on that property. What are you doing Bartholomew? I dread calling you back, but I need your assistance again.

Brooke dials a familiar voice.

"Well, hello again, Miss Hannah." said Chief Jared. "Now either you just really enjoy my conversation, or you're looking for a favor."

"Hello again, chief. Well, I suppose it's both." she said as they both chuckle. "About ten days ago you gave me permission to go inside the Gainsborough house. Well... I need to go back one more time."

"What are you up to young lady? If you're looking for story material to re-circulate this whole mess, I advise you to tread lightly. The last thing I need is having the governor on my head. What are you looking for?"

"I believe Thaddeus may have left us some clues on his true motives behind the killings. I promise I'm not trying to do police work here. In closing out this story, I just want to make sure I've looked at this from all angles. If I do find anything, I promise to turn it over right away."

"Brooke, I gotta tell you, something seems a bit stinky about this whole thing, but I would never question your integrity. We are spread rather thin right now. I could have someone go back out there with you on Monday if that's OK?"

"Yes, it is chief, and thank you again for everything you've done. There will be closure on this very soon."

"I sure hope so. I will have one of my guys contact you early Monday morning. I will let the two of you work out the logistics. Oh, and you'll be quite happy to know that the house has been completely cleaned. It's no longer a crime scene. The place smells like a normal house should."

"Wait a minute! What did they clean chief? Did they throw away anything?"

"Well, that certainly got your dander going didn't it? They basically cleaned that place with industrial solvents to disinfect and sanitize it. The only thing that was discarded was the carpet in the basement. Hopefully you weren't looking for that!?"

Brooke breathes a silent sigh of relief. "No that's perfect! At least I won't have to have my eyes watering like they did last time. That was the most awful smell I've experienced. I will be awaiting the phone call on Monday."

"Very well! Let's hope this gives you what you're looking for to wrap this thing up. Good day Brooke!"

Brooke is optimistic. There was never a mention of any hidden rooms. If everything is still in place, this might give her the upper hand she's been looking for. Either that, or this is just what Milk was expecting of her.

Chapter 36

The Spotlight

Monday June 1, 2015 9:05am

H ello this is Brooke speaking!" She said as she blindly answers the phone with her Bluetooth headset.

"Good morning Brooke, this is Chief Jared. I'm calling you from another line within the building. Say listen, I have a hot button this morning that's going to require some additional personnel. Would it be fine if I had someone escort you to the Gainsborough property sometime this afternoon?"

"Sure chief. That would be great. You're helping me out with this one, so I'm at your disposal."

"Very good. I will have one of my men contact you sometime early this afternoon."

As Brooke and Charlie continue their working on a story development from the news van, Milk is making plans of his own.

10:00am

"Today is the day you've all been waiting for," said Milk to the four hostages. "You want to have your pathetic lives spared, do you? Well, your individual fates are in the hands of someone I truly admire. If she feels any compassion for any of you, perhaps she will find a way to help you. If not, you will suffer miserably and slowly.

"Now, you all remember what you're supposed to say right?" All four of them nod their heads in agreeance. "Good. Well, let's get this show on the road. This is going to be a blast. Let's make that phone call first."

He takes out his cell phone and dials a number.

"It's you!" said Brooke, as her voice slightly cracks.

She steps away from Charlie and the news van to take the call.

"Top of the morning to you, Brooke. I hope you had a great breakfast. You're going to need all your energy. Tell me, are you near some place with a television? There's something I want you to watch."

Here we go again.

"I have access to a television. What are you doing?"

"You are about to see just that in a few moments. Please go to your nearest television and let me know once you're there."

Brooke goes back to the news van. As much as she tries to maintain her composure, Charlie can tell that she's rattled. He doesn't interrupt her as she hops into the back of the van.

"Charlie, can you pull up our station channel? I need the live broadcast."

"Sure thing." Charlie pulls up the live news feed of the morning show on Bay 9.

"I have access. What am I supposed to do now? What channel?"

"That's wonderful to hear. Any channel will do for my little play. I am going to disconnect the call. In two minutes, your life will change drastically. I hope you're ready for this." He disconnects the call.

Brooke slowly turns to Charlie.

"I'm not sure what's about to happen, but I will try to explain everything I promise."

"I'm here for you Brooke and you know that. Please tell me what you…"

The monitor flickers.

"We interrupt this broadcast to bring you a special report."

Brooke's eyes nearly fall to the back of her head. The voice is Milk's. He is patched into the news station and doing a live broadcast. The screen changes to a room that Brooke has become all too familiar with. All four of the hostages are sitting in the same chairs next to one another. This time however, the speaker is sitting in a taller chair directly behind them and centered. The live relay appears to be shot in HD, as you can see all the intricate details of fright and pain on each of the hostage's faces.

"Good morning, everyone, and thank you for taking time out of your busy schedules to join me for a rather important announcement." said Milk as stands.

"I have four people who would like to introduce themselves to you. OK students, one by one. Please make me proud!"

"My name is Maria Delphine. My number is one and my shape is square. I've been missing from my family since January. I would like my life to be spared. Please help me, Brooke."

"What the…?" Said Charlie as he quickly looks at Brooke before returning his eyes to the screen in complete shock. Brooke's face has turned an unfamiliar shade.

"My name is Darla Forte. My number is two and my shape is round. I've been missing from my family since January. I would like my life to be spared. Please help me, Brooke."

"My name is Curtis Lanker. My number is three and my shape is rectangular. I've been missing from my family since February. I would like my life to be spared. Please help me, Brooke."

"My name is Brendon Skiles. My number is four and my shape is triangular. I've been missing from my family since February. I would like my life to be spared. Please help me, Brooke."

"Brooke what the hell is this? Who is this?" asked Charlie.

Brooke is too stunned to speak. Before she can gather her faculties, Milk continues.

"Unfortunately, one of my students couldn't make the trip. She is permanently, shall we say, dismissed. These people have all failed you and they so utterly disgust me. They are like a vile disease that threatens the very foundation of that which we hold dear to us. These diseases hold no moral or tangible significance. They must be eradicated.

"In 36 hours, I will end class for these four ungrateful students. Please rest assured when I tell you they will feel pain like no human being has ever experienced. And all of you will get to witness every last second of it.

"Each of my students have reached out to someone in the 11th hour for help... Brooke Hannah.

Brooke turns and looks at Charlie.

"I'm sorry!"

"Brooke is the only person that I hold in high regard right now. The only other two are dead and gone. She is the one person that understands me. She understands my motivations. She understands my pain. And now it's time to put it all together.

"Brooke, you have 36 hours to figure out this conundrum, though you're already well on your way. I do apologize for putting you in the spotlight, but this is where you were meant to be. Lives are at stake… you better hurry up!

"And, that folks completes my hacking of your Emergency Broadcasting System, and all other systems you thought were masterfully hidden behind those ridiculous firewalls. I assure you this is not a test. You may now go back to your regularly scheduled programming. And Brooke, I'll be in touch… Good day!"

Brooke hunches over quickly, her body trying to reject what she just heard and thought. Her phone rings seconds later, but she doesn't answer. She doesn't even take out her phone to look at the caller id. Her mind and voice are completely paralyzed. Her phone rings again and this time she sends it directly to voicemail. It rings a third time; she clicks the Bluetooth answer button on her headset without saying a word.

"Hello! Hello! Brooke, its Det. Engler. Please we have to talk. You are about to get hit with a shit storm of ---"

She hands the phone to Charlie. She is pale and completely decomposed.

"Hello this is Charlie!"

"Charlie, Det. Engler. Is she OK? Don't answer that, dumb question. Where are you two? I need to get her somewhere safe and quickly."

"We're right up the street from Northeast High School. I don't understand what's going on, detective. Brooke is...... what do you want me to do?"

"Jump on 62nd and head back towards 611. I will meet you two in between."

Charlie jumps in the front seat and pulls off.

"Hang in there Brooke. We're going to sort through this mess together. I'm here for you."

"Why me Charlie? How in the hell did this guy choose me? I don't want to play this game anymore."

"I know you don't. There is a lot for me to learn about this story Brooke, but I will help you through this. Det. Engler will know what to do."

"I don't know. I have to save them. B -- But I don't know how."

Brooke zones back into her thoughts, totally oblivious to everything else including her phone, which has been ringing nonstop. She takes off her headset and places it in her purse.

Charlie sees Det. Engler's car as he flashes the red and blues once. He quickly exits his car and makes his way to the news van.

"Thank you, Charlie." said Det. Engler.

"Yeah, no problem. Now what do we do? The station is going crazy right now. They are blowing up both of our phones."

"The world as we know it stopped in Florida twenty minutes ago. Brooke, I gotta get you out of here. There is no way you can go back home right now. I already spoke with the chief, who has already spoken with the mayor and governor. This craziness is spreading fast."

"The governor!?" said Brooke, as she quickly re-engages. "How does the governor know about something that happened at the station so quickly?"

"You two don't know do you? Damn. It wasn't just your station. That crazy ass broadcasted all over the state. People are blowing up our phones too. They want answers we don't have. By this time tomorrow, we will probably have press from all over the country. Let's get you outta here now."

"OK!" said Brooke as she exits the news van. "Charlie, I will be fine. Keep your phone on. I promise I will call you later. I'm sorry about all of this."

"Nonsense." said Charlie. "You are so strong for battling this nightmare. I will always be here for you. Two peas in a pod. Detective, please take good care of my girl. I wish you both the best."

The detective and Brooke make haste and quickly take off.

"Where are we going detective?"

"Somewhere safe for right now. The chief and mayor will meet us there. We need a plan, and we need it fast. The clock is ticking."

Chapter 37

Strategy Session

Detective Engler takes Brooke to a safe house the department uses in Palmetto. The home located on 8th Street sits back unassuming from the road. Brooke's mind wants to shut down and fail her, but she won't let it. She knows there is too much at stake. There are people that desperately need her.

"Well, here we are," said the detective. "It's not much, but you will be completely safe here. We won't have to worry about anyone dropping by to visit you. Come on, let's go inside."

As the detective and Brooke make their way inside the home, her cell phone continues to buzz continuously in her purse.

"My phone has been going bananas since that telecast. I have to check my messages detective."

"Understood. But if you receive a phone call from any numbers you don't know, be extra cautious. It could be members of the press trying to get an inside scoop. Your cell number is out there in cyberspace where anyone who really wants to can retrieve it. And God forbid if they could also somehow track the signal.

"Oh, and if that lunatic calls, I need you to put me up to the phone. We need to get a location on that place. Do you know where he might be?"

"I haven't a clue. He calls me randomly, and it's always quiet in the background. He told me in the very beginning that his cell phone was untraceable, and not to bother."

"I guess we'll have to see about that. We have a lot to discuss. The chief and mayor should be here shortly. They will be in an unmarked Cherokee. They can pull into the garage, and no one will suspect a thing."

Brooke takes out her phone and looks at her display in amazement. "I have 27 missed calls and 8 voicemails! Oh no… No!"

"What's wrong?"

"My dad has called me twice and sent me two text messages checking on me. How is it possible that he knows all the way in Detroit?"

"Welcome to the other side of the fence. News like this travels at the speed of light. I sure hope he didn't broadcast outside of Florida, this place will truly become a nightmare.

"My station manager called me. I have to call him back. I owe him an explanation."

As Brooke calls her station manager, the detective thinks, *Hell! You owe me and explanation.*

"Hello Mr. Bergdoll." Her voice is off-balanced and animated. "I'm so sorry sir. I should have come to you at the beginning, but I was afraid… I"

"Slow down Brooke," said Mr. Bergdoll. "Charlie has already spoken with me. I'm glad you are safe. Your name went from local to national in the span of half an hour. I believe you broke some records today young lady. The chief already called me. I know he's on his way to see you. That was quick thinking on their behalf's to get you away from here. Charlie says he has an emergency key to your house, is that correct?"

"Yes sir, it will open all of the doors. He also has an alarm code."

"OK, I will take care of everything here. Don't worry, we will get through this thing together, and quickly. You did the right thing. Never doubt yourself. I will be by there this evening to see you. We will talk then."

Brooke hangs up the phone and checks her voicemail. There are two messages from her dad, one of them with her mom in the background. The rest are from concerned co-workers from the station and her friend Special Agent Lana Quivner.

"Well at least it's from everyone that I do know so far. Detective, without you saying anything, I know you have a million questions circulating through your brain. Let me assure you that I didn't come to you because I didn't want to put those innocent lives at risk. And Bartholomew is not one to toy with. And, I really do appreciate you helping me out back there. If it weren't for you, I'm sure I would be in a sea of reporters. I guess I truly appreciate the saying "And now the teacher becomes the student.""

"Listen Brooke, I have lots of questions surrounding this whole catastrophe. We will have our time soon. But first things first. Mayor Braden and Chief Jared just pulled up and in the garage."

The mayor and chief enter the house through the side attached garage entrance, as Brooke and Detective Engler meet them in the dining room.

"Brooke, I don't know what to say," said the chief. "What in the hell did we witness today? This story is breaking news all around the country, and you're at the center of it. If that ain't damn ironic, I don't know what is. We need a bead on this psycho immediately. What can you tell us about him?"

"Brooke, if I may." said the mayor. "Our city is in utter confusion and dismay. The governor and I have spoken with the families of the four hostages personally. They are obviously beside themselves right now. I know this must be unfathomable for you right now, but you are the only one that can help us. How does he know you? How long has he been in contact with you? We are here to collectively find answers. And of course, the press is chomping at the bits right now. I'm not sure that there has ever been a spectacle like this before. We're having an emergency press conference tomorrow at the headquarters. Please tell us everything we need to know, Brooke."

"Mayor and chief... and to you also detective, I offer my sincerest apologies. I have been deceitful to you all, though not due to my own intentions. His name is Milk, and yes that's his real name. He also goes by and probably more readily favors, Bartholomew. It's his last name that will ring a bell to you all... Gainsborough!"

"GAINSBOROUGH!?" said both the chief and detective.

"That's right! Thaddeus Gainsborough was his fraternal twin brother.

"How is that possible!? Asked the chief. "We ran a file on Thaddeus the length of a football field and came up with squat. He was as clean as a whistle. He had a successful law practice but was never married. Hell, it doesn't seem as though he ever had a girlfriend.

"We couldn't even find any family history on that guy. It was like he just left the grid and took all his information with him. How do you know the information you have is valid?"

"I learned most of this information over the past few days, chief. He invited me to lunch this past Friday. We sat face to face outside at a busy restaurant where he was totally out of place yet blended in just the same.

"He poured out his heart to me. I think he wants me to know everything about him. For what reason, I am still a bit cloudy. One night, Cinco de Mayo as a matter of fact, I received a strange phone call. I didn't recognize the voice, and I thought it was some sort of prank call. He kept telling me he lost something. Well, eventually he lost his patience with me. He told me he lost his tea pot and that maybe my next door neighbor could help me find it. That's the night my neighbor, Mr. Gregory, passed away.

"He was sitting on my front porch in the swing with an empty teapot sitting in his lap. I learned that Bartholomew was camped out watching my house from a distance. He saw Mr. Gregory collapse in the yard, while no doubt on his way to see me. He picked him up and placed him in my swing.

"After speaking with Detective Engler, I was convinced that the person that called had nothing to do with Mr. Gregory's death, that they probably wouldn't show their face anywhere near me again. But the next day he called me again. He basically told me I was going to play his game and at no time must I ever involve any outsiders into the equation, especially the police. He said any non-conformance would result in pain unimaginable. He's been feeding me clues ever since.

"Bartholomew is also the one responsible for Ingrid Sellers' death. If we don't execute with perfection, he will kill those people. We have much to discuss gentlemen."

Brooke goes into detail on the videos, Bartholomew's possible motive, and what their next steps might be.

"This story has so many markings of the classic case of abuse." said the chief. "I have seen many cases in my years where the abused becomes the abuser. They long for something they never had, which in this case is love and affection.

"According to those journals you *skillfully* lifted from the house, looks like Mr. Bartholomew has murdered before. We need to find out more about the twin's relationship in these past few years. There may be more bodies out there than we were made to believe.

"I want you and Engler to go back out to that house tomorrow. We need you to show us how to gain entrance to this hidden room. Detective, take another squad car with you for back up."

"Yes sir."

"With our next step identified, we need to prepare for the press conference at 9:00am tomorrow." said the mayor. We have a lot riding on this one."

"About the press conference." said Brooke. "I would like to speak to the reporters. I know their language, and I believe I owe it to the families. People are going to want to hear from me quickly. Will you allow me to take part in it?"

"As much as I want to err to the side of caution and say no," said the mayor. "You might be right. Perhaps having you speak for a few moments will give us another angle we can use to our advantage. What do you think, chief?"

"Agreed! Let's discuss what we want to cover tomorrow."

Chapter 38

Full Court Press

7:30 am the next morning

Brooke sits in the chief's office as she readies herself for an unfamiliar platform. For years she has been the reporter with the microphone extended, jockeying for the best position to ensure her questions were answered. And now she is the object or more appropriately, pawn, in this perverse mystery. She knows she has the respect of her local comrades; however, the national media will more than likely attempt to rip her apart.

"Well Brooke, I think we have this thing down to a science." said the chief. "You are incredibly prepared for this. I'm going to leave you be for a little bit. I will have the detective swing by and get you when we are ready.

"Before that though, there's someone I want you to speak with. Her name is Dr. Joan Lesters. She is one of the best criminal profilers in the country. She is especially skilled with profiling serial killers and rapists. She is a good friend that has offered her services to us. There is no need for a deep in the weed's conversation. We will save that for some time after this conference. For now, she simply wants to meet you and say hello. Is it OK if I bring her in?"

"Sure chief, I will gladly speak with her. Anything that can help this case... I'm all for it."

171

"Great! I will go up front and bring her back. I'll be back in a few moments. We will get through this day, Brooke. And we will find that bastard before he does those people any harm. We are going to get this done together."

"Thank you chief. I appreciate everything you've done for me."

As she awaits the profiler, Brooke reaches for her phone to check her emails, it rings suddenly, which startles her. As she peers at her caller id, her temporary anxiety turns into a smile.

"Hi dad. How are you doing? I'm so glad you called." she said as her heart rate slowed.

"Hi, baby girl. This will be the quickest conversation that you and I have ever had. After your mom and I got off the phone with you last night, we both got on our knees and prayed for you. You got this darling, and we love you. Now please be careful and extra vigilant. If you need us, we are there in a heartbeat. Go get'em!"

Before Brooke could properly say goodbye, her dad disconnected the call. There is a knock on the chief's door.

"Who is it?"

"It's Dr. Lesters."

"Please come in doctor, I was just having a quick chat with my father."

"I'm sure your parents and the rest of your family are completely up in arms over this situation. I must say that you are doing them proud with the way you are handling yourself. Many would have already folded under the pressure."

"Thank you, doctor, I am committed to helping bring this case to a peaceful resolution. The chief speaks highly of you, and says you are a great profiler. What do you think about what you've seen with this case so far?"

"I'm not going to spend much time defining what a serial killer is. We are beyond the description phase. Based on the video and your previous interaction with him, we can safely assume there will be more interactions. Some of what I've seen from the perpetrator fits the perfect serial mold we've created. Serial killers are typically classified in two ways. One is based on motive, while the other is based on organizational and social patterns.

"Not every serial killer falls into a single type, and these classifications don't explain what leads someone to become a serial killer. There is still so much we don't know about this person, and that's what worries me.

"Today, at this critical hour, we don't know who we are dealing with completely. From the video footage we can tell that he is highly capable. He appears to meet the profiling of a process-focused serial killer. They get enjoyment from torture and the death of their victims.

"But there is something else missing that perplexes me, Brooke. I'd like to ask that you share with me any conversations you have with the perpetrator, when we have time for a more extensive conversation. We might be able to establish a pattern and most importantly a motive behind this side show."

There is another knock at the door.

"Who is it?" Asked Brooke.

"It's Detective Engler. You mind if I join you for a moment?"

The detective opens the door.

173

"Oh, I'm sorry I didn't realize you had… well, good morning Dr. Lesters. It's nice to see you again."

"Good morning detective. Please come in. Brooke and I were just having a chat. We are all done for now. Please take my card and let me know if I can help you in any way. I'm sure we will be speaking again soon."

"Thank you for your time, doctor."

The doctor makes her exit, closing the door behind her.

"Good morning, detective."

"Good morning to you. Well, we have about ten minutes before the press conference starts. The chief is going to kick things off. Before we go out there, I wanted to tell you something."

"Sure, please tell me what's on your mind."

"When I invited you to lunch and we talked more about the Ingrid Sellers case, I could tell that there was something off kilter, yet I couldn't lay a finger on it. And full disclosure, I even had a conversation with the chief about it.

"After seeing this whole thing come to light, and hearing everything you told us last night, I want to let you know that I deeply respect you for what you did. I can't imagine what you've been going through, but I promise we will solve this case and save those people. Now, it's time for you to go out there and make a symphony out of this circus."

9:00am

Due to the sheer number of reporters, the chief holds the news conference in the parking lot across from the station. As alluded to, there are reporters from around the country in attendance.

"Good morning." said the chief. "I thank all of you for coming. I especially appreciate the families for being here. I know this has been rough on all of you. I'm going to keep this conference brief, as we have a lot of work ahead of us.

"Everyone saw the video clip yesterday. Such a thing is truly unprecedented. In all my years in law enforcement, I have seen many things, but this one is unique and rare.

"Yesterday we had someone challenge the very thing that we hold dear to us... That's our freedom, and we will not let *anyone* take that away from us. Everything in that submission is being carefully and judiciously worked by my department. We know a great deal more about the hostages thanks to the families involved. And we also have identified the perpetrator in the video.

"My department will not rest until we have saved those four victims and have the person responsible for kidnapping them in our custody. These individuals will be free again. I know many if not all of you have questions about Brook Hannah's involvement with this case. I'm going to have her speak with you briefly. Before I bring her up, I'm going to open it up for some questions."

"Chief. Sander Gleeson, Boston Globe. This person in the video has had these hostages for months now. What was the significance of broadcasting this information yesterday? And why across the state? What's the story behind his message?"

"At this point we don't know the significance of launching his video yesterday. This is another angle we are investigating.

The same goes for what his message is or isn't. Rest assured that my department will resolve this quickly."

"Chief. Anthony Baxter, WDIV Detroit. What can you tell us about the man in the video? Is he a local resident? Didn't you find it odd how the victims in the video behaved?"

"The only thing I can share about the man in the video is that we know his name and are tracing some elements that are key to our investigation. As soon as we can release more information, I will hold another press conference."

"Chief Jared. Anya Spivey, Associated Press. The perpetrator hacked into the most sophisticated systems in the state with relative ease. Do you think this is an inside job? Is someone else helping him?"

"My department is still evaluating how he was able to hack our systems so effectively. At this point, it does not appear to be an inside job. We are still trying to determine if he has any accomplices. Ok, I'm going to bring Brooke Hannah up to have a few words with you."

Brooke makes her way to the platform.

"Good morning to you all." Brooke looks directly at the families of the kidnapped victims. "I know these nearly 24 hours have been incredible, unrealistic, and emotional. I am not here as a spokesperson; however, I feel supremely confident that Chief Jared and his department is doing everything they can to bring closure and a positive ending to this terrifying story.

"I know there are many questions as to how or why I've become central to this case. While I would like nothing more than to provide full disclosure, there are still many things I don't understand myself. But please rest assured that I am working with Chief Jared to do whatever I can.

"I suppose I don't have much I can add that the chief has not already articulated. I know that you might have some questions for me, so I'd like to open it up now."

Brooke marvels at how well her counterparts navigate and influence their way for optimal positioning. The first face she picks is a familiar one.

"Brooke. Kirsten Lawry, Bay 9 News. The guy in the video specifically called you out. The hostages all begged you to save them. How do you know this person and how are *you* going to prevent this?"

"I didn't know who this was until approximately 30 days ago. He contacted me by phone. I don't know how he got my information. The context of our conversations and what they mean are being actively worked by this police department. I can assure you that I will do whatever I can in my capacity to help resolve this situation."

The reporters go into an absolute frenzy. There is a sea of flashes, microphones, and pleading drowning out Brooke's senses. She points to a random reporter.

"Craig Singletary, USA Today. You stated that you didn't know who the perpetrator in the video was until approximately 30 days ago. How did you meet him? Was he a blind date? Are you romantically involved with him? Is that why you can't tell us who he is?"

Chief Jared feels compelled to end the remainder of the questions. He doesn't like the direction they are going; however, he has complete confidence in her. Brooke is well poised and particular in her response.

"Thank you for your question, Mr. Singletary. Allow me to add some clarity to my previous statement. My first interaction with this man was through a phone call to my cell phone late one night. Prior to that call, I had never communicated with him. And there is no romantic interest. I am working with Chief Jared giving him any information I have so all the possible angles can be vetted out expeditiously... Next question."

"Brooke. Evan Parker, CNN. With all due respect to the families, our sources have confirmed that all four hostages had cases opened with Child Protective Services. Were you aware of that?"

"No, Mr. Parker I was not. I..."

"We also have credible sources that state you broke your arm during a softball game in tenth grade. Was it the softball game that broke your arm, or was it abuse from your parents? Is that the reason this man has reached out to you?"

This question completely catches Brooke off guard. Not only is her counterpart questioning her integrity, but he has also brought her parents into the mix. She stumbles for a moment as the camera flashes temporarily stifle her.

The chief quickly rises to take over the mic and end the press conference. Brooke gestures him to stand down as she looks directly at the questioning reporter.

"Mr. Parker, you have brought to light some compelling information. I'm sure the chief and his department will likely want to speak with you more about what you've stated concerning the Child Protective Services cases." Brooke then looks into the sea of other reporters. "I implore all of you to please do the same. If you have any information that might aid this department in this case, please come forward after this conference. As far as my arm. It is true that I broke it trying to steal second base and *failing* miserably." she said with a smile.

There are chuckles amongst the crowd, which loosens the tension in the air.

"My parents have given me many things. Most important amongst them are love, respect, and continuous support. It has been that way since I was born, and it has never wavered. I thank you all for your questions and for attending this press conference. With your help, we can collectively work to put an end to this menace."

"Brooke, one more question …!"

She quickly exits the platform and walks back inside the station with Detective Engler. The chief closes the press conference and meets them both back in his office.

"Brooke, I gotta tell you I like how you handled yourself up there." said the chief. "Those weren't easy questions at all. And when that one jackass accused your parents of abusing you, I wanted to strangle him for you. You certainly showed a different side of you today. I believe you helped to lay certain questions to rest, but so many still remain."

"I was informed from my good friend and your station manager, Mr. Bergdoll that they were giving you some paid time off in the aftermath of these events."

"Yes, that's true sir. He wants me to assist you in any way I can. We don't have much time."

"Indeed, we don't. I want you to go with the detective and find that hidden room. There's just got to be something there that can help us. And detective, I'm sure you're already thinking the same thing, but I want you back out at Mrs. Gainsborough house. I'm thinking the conversation will go much differently this time around. Let's base our timeline on what you find out today; not that we have much of one anyway."

Chapter 39

Special Delivery

The air in Florida is full of freshly manicured lawns and landscaping, yet the atmosphere is suffocating the day after the news flash heard across the country. There is one person who is totally oblivious to the chaos. The doorbell rings.

"Who is it?"

"Hello, its Darren from the leasing office. I have a delivery for you that was sent to us by mistake. Is this Abigail Gainsborough?"

"What kind of delivery? I didn't order anything."

Darren is pleasant yet aggravated that she won't just open the door.

"Yes ma'am, understood. It is a bouquet of flowers with two envelopes attached to it."

"Well, I didn't order any flowers, so I don't want them."

"I'm just going to leave them here against your door. Have a great day." he said as he walked away... *Weird ass!*

Abigail covertly shuffles her blinds to see he had walked away. She slightly cracked her door and surely enough sees a nice arrangement of flowers neatly wrapped in white paper. She decides to take them as she carefully surveils her surroundings. Paranoia had become a great friend.

As she carefully removes the white paper, her skepticism turns into a smile, as she has never seen a more beautiful arrangement of flowers. They are exotic and unfamiliar. She places them on the dining room table and adds water to them, as they are already in a rather nice crystal vase.

She anxiously opens the first card and reads it:

"If you want strong bones, you can never have too much Milk"

What the hell is this?

She quickly glances again at the front of the envelope, and surely enough it's made out to her directly.

This makes no damn sense.

She opens the second envelope, unfolds a piece of paper, and stares at the picture enclosed. It's a dark circle centered on the paper. It gave the appearance of something a frustrated child may have drawn. It just repeats itself over again with precision.

There is a faint scribble of words at the bottom that say, I hate you.

What kind of bull ----

There is another knock at the door.

"What is it now?" Abigail shouted.

"My apologies. There is a box that goes with the rest of these things." he said.

"What's in the damn box?" she asked, as she opens the front door with force and fury.

"Hello mama. The box is empty, but your head belongs in it. Let's get it off you."

Chapter 40

This Old House

Brooke, Detective Engler, and another unmarked squad car arrive at the Gainsborough residence. Brooke realizes her purpose for being here this time around is just as cloudy as the previous. She hopes the clarity she seeks lie hidden behind the wall.

"So, do you know if Bartholomew and Thaddeus stayed here together exclusively?" asked the detective. "The name on the deed was never changed from the doctor that owned this place."

"He never made that clear. They reunited at some point after Bartholomew arrived. That's as much as I know."

"Alright, you ready?"

"Yes, I'm ready. I hope this isn't a dead end. Let's go in."

The detective instructs the other officer to secure the perimeter and standby for backup if needed. As Brooke enters the house, the first thing she notices is the non-existence of the pungent and reverberating smells that ruled the air the last time. They have all but disappeared.

"Wow! They did a nice job of cleaning up that disgusting smell. The basement is this way, detective."

"OK, lead the way."

Brooke finds the light switch which brilliantly lights their descent. As they make their way into the basement, it's completely empty. The previous furniture was not salvageable.

There is but one single painting on the wall that stands out. Upon further inspection.

"This is it!" said Brooke excitedly. "*Basement Therapy* is the name of the picture."

She motions with her hand pointing to the picture on the wall.

"If you remove it, there should be a keyhole of some sort."

"OK," he said, as he removes the picture frame from the wall. "I'll be damned. I guess he was telling you the truth after all. But wait a minute, what about the key?"

"It must be around here somewhere I…"

"Wait a minute, Brooke, I think we got something here."

He flips the picture frame to the rear. Affixed it is an envelope marked, *Brooke*.

"This sick bastard is toying with us. He knows our every move. I wouldn't be surprised if he's watching us right now. Based on everything that's happened so far, I'm going to have to assume it's safe to open the envelope, but just in case, let me have at it first."

The detective opens the envelope away from his body, praying there's no anthrax or any other surprises.

"OK, I think we're good. You want to read the note inside?"

Brooke takes the envelope and unfolds the letter. A small key drops to the floor.

"Well, I believe this is our key," she said as the detective picks it up. "I don't understand what this means, but I don't like it. It says to head back upstairs and take two wrapped steaks from the refrigerator with us. It warns us not to proceed further without them."

"You gotta be kidding me. I believe this is about to get interesting. Let's go back upstairs together."

They go to the refrigerator and surely enough there are two uncooked steaks wrapped in paper.

"I don't like this one-bit, Brooke. These steaks look quite fresh to me. That psycho has been here recently. It's no telling what he may have done to this house. It could be rigged with explosives or God knows what else. I think we should come back with more resources."

"Detective, if it were anyone else, we were talking about, I would quickly agree. I can't explain it, but I don't think he wants to harm us. He needs us to finish this quest he's set up in his mind. I think he's opening the doors for us. It's up to us to figure out where they lead. Please, let's just continue."

"You make a great point. Let's just make it quick. Surprises aren't a policeman's best friend."

They return to the basement where the detective inserts the key in the hole on the wall.

"OK Brooke, from here on out I want you to stay on my heels. Who the hell knows what we'll encounter once inside? I hope I don't have to use this." he said as he brandishes his firearm.

He turns the key and like magic a click is heard, and a seam is exposed in the far wall. Whatever lies behind this entrance has been exempted from the cleanliness of the surrounding house. There is a smell of blood and something badly decayed. As they get nearer to the entrance, the sound of flies orchestrates chaos and depravity. The detective draws his Sig Sauer ready for what lies ahead.

"This smell is unbearable." said the detective. "Here, I brought us some supplies just in case. Let's put these masks and gloves on. We don't need to inhale this garbage, and we sure as hell don't need to make skin contact with anything. Here we go, Brooke."

He opens the hidden door and surprisingly sees a light switch. When he flips the switch, what they see takes their breath away.

Chapter 41

The Hidden Surprise

What the hell is this place?" said the detective. "What was he using this place for? Brooke, some of this... the blood looks recent."

The detective and Brooke pan the room from the left to right. It is a 20x20 fully finished room with thirteen hospital beds lined up like soldiers next to one another. The sheets on each bed have blood stains strewn about them; some more than others. The four beds on the right appear to have more recent blood stains. There are charts hanging on the wall atop each bed. There are also numerous charts, notes, and pictures in near perfect order on the far-left wall. The chaotic hum of flies is deafening.

"Detective, those flies are not in this room. It's coming from behind that wall."

He temporarily holsters his weapon sensing no immediate danger.

"That's strange." he said as he walks towards the wall and knocks. "It's hollow, Brooke! I betcha there's another room behind this one. The one we probably don't want to see. First things first. Let's see what we can uncover in here."

"How about I start on the far wall reading through those notes?"

"Sounds good, I will read through these patient charts to see what this bastard was doing."

Brooke approaches the wall and immediately gravitates to the pictures. There are thirteen pictures hanging. As she glances at each, the last five strike a familiar chord.

"Detective, these pictures... five of them I recognize. It's Ingrid Sellers and the other four missing people from his telecast."

"What? Let me see those," he said as he scans the pictures. "Brooke, the other people. These people are the ones that Thaddeus killed. I remember these faces well, especially the governor's niece. We executed him for killing these people. He confessed. I don't understand this. Did we have the wrong person?"

"Look at this." said Brooke. "It's a diagram. Wait a minute." She opens a manila file folder clipped to the wall marked *Marionette 2.0*. There are four full pages of progress notes. She continues to read.

"Detective, he picked up where Dr. Ronald Saflin left off. He looked up to the doctor. He has brought the doctor's vision to life. The marionette name makes complete sense now. This details how he implanted the devices in Ingrid's body. And it's just like you thought. He is able to control them with a type of central remote. He's controlling these people like puppets. That's probably what these beds were for. What do the charts say?"

The detective goes back to the first bed on the left.

"It doesn't look like he used any device on this first victim. It looks like he was experimenting with various types of anesthesia. The same for the next person too."

As he continues from left to right, it's the same pattern for the first eight victims. The chart on the ninth bed belongs to

Ingrid Sellers and is consistent with what they discovered. The next four charts are the same except for one small detail from Ingrid's chart.

"This is interesting," said the detective. "Our current victims all have the same devices embedded and wired through their bodies. But they also have some type of device like a small receptacle where he places a needle and administers medicine. It looks like he's keeping them doped up as well."

"Detective, I have something else. You're not going to believe this, but Thaddeus was not only his brother, he was a patient."

Chapter 42

Research Assistant

December 27, 2011

Thaddeus, we have both lived entire lifetimes it seems," said Bartholomew as he and his brother sit in front of the fireplace of their new home. I wish the doctor was still living. You would have truly appreciated his character and odd sense of humor. Besides you, he was the only other person who never judged me. His work was so important yet misunderstood by so many, kind of like me.

"The research he was working on would change the way we look at medicine today. The technological advances were numerous, but they were overshadowed by doubt and fear. The world agonizes on how quickly we can advance, yet when it's smacked in the face by progress, the world retreats.

"He taught me a great deal. I know more than many of these crackpot doctors. And my technological expertise, I believe cannot be rivaled. But who would listen to me? I have no degrees, I have no connections, and I have no history. To the world I don't exist, all thanks to our dear parents. His work deserves a voice, and I intend to give it one."

"What do you have in mind brother," asked Thaddeus. "I have to agree that you are off the grid. But surely placing your past back together is not too difficult a task. You could certainly get your GED and quickly go through college. Based on your aptitude, there are many things you can test out of. I'm sure that you could have a degree in two years if you really wanted it. But I'm sensing if that were the case, you'd have already done it. Tell me, what is it that you are planning?"

"I've already started the research. I've been using myself as the test subject, but I can only go so far. This is not the type of research where I can play dual roles. I need to find actual subjects that would gladly volunteer for what will be groundbreaking results. This is where I'm stuck. I was thinking …"

"Use me then." said Thaddeus. "Let me help you with your research. I would be honored to be a part of this. I am so proud of you for how far you've come. Please let me help."

"Absolutely not. Trying it on myself is one thing, I can't have you going through… no Thaddeus, I just can't. I will find another way."

"You are the person closest to me, and it has always been that way. Even when mom and dad tried to keep us separated, I always felt you. I hurt for you. I agonized for you. And as we sit here tonight, I can feel the passion run through you like a wildfire. I place my complete trust in you, dear brother. I realize there are risks associated with this. If I can help you help others, I'm all for it."

"I don't know about this. The phase of the research that you would have to undergo might possibly have you on bedrest for days or weeks even. What about your practice? You can't be a lawyer going through these medical trials."

"My practice is in good hands with Kermit. He can take care of things until I return. So, when do I start?"

Against his intuition, Bartholomew allowed his brother to aid him in his research. There were two phases that needed to be vetted out to prove his additional assumptions or theories. Thaddeus would have to undergo neurological and physiological changes.

The first two weeks of testing and assimilation went much better than anticipated. Thaddeus was proving to be the perfect subject. The third week brought about unexpected results.

"OK Thaddeus, we are back in recovery. You did outstanding. I can't wait to show you the results. At this rate, I will have enough data in one month to apply for funding. You were right. I'm going to do it the right way and take the time necessary to see this through. If that means getting my GED and then going through college to pay my dues, then I'm all for it. The doctor will smile upon us. I will just need you for one more..."

"I would love a soda, Bartholomew. Do you have the red kind? Oh, and can I have some ice cream too? I've been good today, haven't I?"

"Umm sure, brother. Whatever you want. I think the meds are still in your system. Just sit back and relax."

"I love riding horses, don't you, Bartholomew? Hey, I know. Do you think we can get some horses to ride here? I promise to take care of them. Please!"

"Sure, Thaddeus, we can get some horses."

He said as he is perplexed on his brother's condition.

Why is he acting like this!? I used the same dosage as last time. Nothing is different. 35cc of... "Oh, God. Nooo!"

"What's wrong, Bartholomew? Are you upset that you don't know which ice cream to pick? I like cookies and cream. Or how about rum raisin, yummy."

In a flash, Bartholomew's life flashed before his eyes. After all the planning and exceptionally specific preparation, he forgot the one thing that was most important. The medicine, Kurvacta, which is used to create hallucinations, must never exceed 20cc at its highest dose. He mistakenly gave his brother 35cc. It was enough to partially fry his brain; thereby, leaving him in a state of incalculable euphoria.

In one fell swoop, his brother and his research went down the drain. But that would soon change.

Chapter 43

The Work of Evil

So he never meant to hurt his brother after all," said Brooke. "He made a terrible mistake. There's more in here. It looks like he felt really bad about everything that happened. He vowed to take care of his brother for the rest of their lives. He goes on to say that the research consumed him at this point. He realized he had to continue, no matter what. There's nothing else here that really makes any sense."

"Brooke. Look over there. Don't you find it a bit odd that there's only one picture on these walls. Stands out like the last one doesn't it."

"It sure does. Well, let's see what's behind it."

The detective removes the painting from the wall and sure enough, there's a note affixed behind it.

"OK, you're gonna love this one." said the detective. "It says we should listen to something under the pillow of bed #3. This is really getting annoying, Brooke."

They walk beside and flank the third bed. The detective carefully moves the pillow aside and discovers a tape recorder, a file folder, and a remote control.

"Well let's see what it says." said the detective as he awkwardly pressed play.

"Hello Brooke. I'm glad you have made it to this point. There is something else you need to understand, and it's behind this wall. I left you

some data in that folder. It's a great read. There is so much to discover yet so little time. Send Robert my best! And don't forget to take those tasty steaks with you. They're going to come in handy."

"Brooke, have a look inside and tell me what this nut is talking about."

Brooke grabs the folder marked Project Bob and scampers through the six pages of data.

"After the accident with his brother, he was ready to give up on the research. He was deeply depressed, but at the same time he was bitter, extremely bitter. He blamed everything that happened on the two people he hated most, his mother and father. Through his hatred he bore a new idea, one he called, *radical and necessary.*

"The rest of this pertains to dosages of medicines I've never heard of. He lists many of them as anti-inflammatory medicines. He ends it with welcome to Project RG."

"I don't know what any of that means." said the detective, "but I believe we're about to find out."

He clicks the single button on the remote control, and like magic the wall directly behind the bed collapses to the floor. In a flurry, hundreds of flies angrily appear from the musty shadows and quickly blind the light in the room. Many of them leave the room via the first entrance, while the rest retreat back into the dark hole. The smell is heartbreaking and familiar. The detective and Brooke replace their paper masks with specially equipped gas masks that he brought along for this type of need.

The detective draws his weapon as the repulsion of flies eventually gives way to another light switch on the wall. As he reaches for the switch…

"Don't do that! Stay away from that." said a mangled and desperate voice. "It will hurt my eyes terribly."

"Who the hell is that?" asked the detective. "Show your face or we're about to have some problems. Show your face now, with your hands up where I can see them."

"Please don't hurt me mister. I mean no harm. I can't walk. He took my feet. Please, I'm so hungry. I have my urine to drink, but I need food. Please be so kind mister!"

The detective is tense and steadfast.

"Who the hell are you? Why are you here?"

The detective aims his flashlight into the path of the voice. What he sees makes him drop his firearm to his side in shock. Brooke nearly collapses.

An elderly man sits stabilized against the wall. There is a metal cuff attached to his wrist with a thick and heavy chain bound to the wall. He has but inches to move around. There is a fully functional sink and toilet directly in front of him, yet they are both outside of his reach. Its obvious Bartholomew wanted to humiliate this man. There is simply no way to tell how long this man has been in this basement room. His pants have been loaded with so much feces and urine, that they have become a part of his body makeup.

As the detective pans his light down the man's legs, he sees that both of his feet had been cut off. Judging by the precision of the cuts, they were probably surgically removed. Upon closer inspection, the detective can see the man's teeth while somewhat rotted, have been filed down into sharp instruments of cutting torture.

"Mister, I beg of you, I'm so hungry. Please give me something to eat. He has not fed me in four days."

"Detective." Brooke whispered. "Do you think that's what these steaks are for?"

"Yeah maybe. You're probably right. I tell you what old man. If I give you something to eat, you have to tell me everything you know about this place. And I want to know everything about who you are and who did this to you."

"I promise to tell you everything I know. Please give me some food."

"First, who else is in here with you?"

"No one. I am alone."

The detective throws the two raw steaks to the man as he quickly devours both. The man reaches for the cup directly beside him to drink.

"Hey, wait a minute." said the detective. "What's in that cup?"

"It's my urine. It's the only thing he allows me to drink. Maybe once a week, he will give me water to drink, but it's never clean. He is a cruel boy."

"Don't drink that!" shouted the detective in revulsion. "Brooke, look right behind us on that table over there. Can you dump out the cotton balls? I will fill that up with some fresh water."

The detective fills the glass container with fresh water from the sink. He sets it down within reach of the man, as he watches him quickly devour it. The man slides the glass jar back to the detective asking for more to which he obliges. The man is thankful, yet he is still weak. His voice is slow and controlled.

"Who are you?" asked the detective. "How long have you been here?"

"My name is Robert and I've been here for a very long time. I don't know how long anymore. I miss my wife. He brought her by to visit me just this morning. I hated for her to see me like this. He made her watch me. He used that damn device thing. When he uses it I can't control myself anymore. He made me chew holes in my arm. It always hurts so badly. He just laughed at me as my wife cried. He's going to hurt her. I begged him to stop. Can you help us? Don't let him harm her please. You're the police, right? Won't you do something?"

"Who did this to you? Who is your wife?"

"Milk did this. He's no son of mine. My wife's name is Abigail."

"Abigail!? Abigail Gainsborough?" said Brooke as she now stands beside the detective. "She said you were dead."

The detective looks perplexed as he pieces together what he's just heard.

"How do you know my wife? You can save her then?"

"Wait a minute." said the detective. "You said you saw your wife this morning?"

"Yes, that's right. He has her. You must help her."

The detective turns to Brooke. They realize Bartholomew is once again one step ahead of them. After all these years, they wonder what he's planning for his mother.

"We want to help you, but you have to help us first. How did you get here? Where is your son now?"

"He tricked me. That's how he got me here. It was never a secret that Abigail and I never had much in terms of money. Our boy Thaddeus took great care of us once he became a really good lawyer.

"But I had a love for gambling. I liked the blackjack table specifically. I won here and there, but nothing ever major. Sometimes I would get one of those cards I could use for free hotel stays and restaurants. Abigail didn't care much for it, but she was just fine with me going once a week.

"One day I received this call from a guy at the Seminole Hard Rock Casino in Tampa. He told me they made a mistake with my last comp calculations and was giving me credit for $500.00 in casino credit for the inconvenience. That just about blew my mind. They told me I could pick up a new card from their promotions agent. He would be set up at the local Holiday Inn. I didn't think anything of it. Hell, I couldn't wait to get my card.

"I went to the hotel the next day and knocked at the door. I was promptly greeted by a face I'd never forget. It was Milk. Before I could react, he hit me with a stun gun. When I woke up I was on a hospital bed. He thanked me for volunteering for his research. He told me I was the perfect assistant. He pumped stuff in me almost daily. I was always high on some type of drug. When he put these damned implants in me, he didn't use any anesthesia. He cleaned my incisions with alcohol and bleach.

"That boy thinks he's a genius, but he's just a sorry loser like he's always been. What he does is not medicine. He is just toying with people's lives for his own amusement. He ruined my poor son, Thaddeus, with this bullshit.

"My poor boy would come down and visit with me from time to time, but it was like speaking with him when he was a young boy most of the time. He couldn't seem to realize the bad things his brother was doing. That bastard took my son's mind away.

"You wanna know where he is? I don't know that answer, but if you want to get to him, you'll need to find a way to knock down that wall. You see, he built up that wall about four months ago. I guess he's been preparing for this day. I don't know who you are young lady, but it's obvious you're a cop there, fella.

"This house is rigged with all sorts of traps. You might want to get some backup and dogs before you come back here.

The detective and Brooke walk over to the far wall feeling around for some type of switch that would cause the wall to reveal a path as one's previous to it.

"Listen, I'm going to get you some medical help." said the detective as he tries his radio. "It's no use, Officer Kennedy can't hear me. These walls are too thick for my signal to penetrate through. Hang tight sir. I will have some help for you soon."

"Wait… Please." said Mr. Gainsborough. I don't want any more medical attention officer. I am ruined. My body is ruined. I have not been able to leave this space for a very long time. How cruel of that boy to place a damn toilet and sink just right outside my reach. Do you know how many times I've had to shit on myself? Do you know how many times I've had to drink piss? My own piss! My legs are full of disgusting sores. It can't be long before my legs have to be cut off. That damn boy would just find another way to keep me going.

"If you want to help me, I'm begging you to do something decent for me, son. I don't want to leave this place. Even If I could make it back to Abigail, there's no way I would want her to see me like this. No one deserves this. Unholster that gun of yours and take me away from this pain. Then go and save my wife, please."

"Sir, I have no idea what hell you've been through, but it stops today. I will get…"

"You're wasting your breath officer. If this were you, would you want to go back? But maybe this will help your decision more."

He turns his back away from the wall and towards the detective. The entire back of his shirt had been cut away. He has deep bruising and gashes across the top of his back.

"Close and cover your eyes sir." asked the detective. "I'm going to flip on this light switch."

Mr. Gainsborough covers his eyes and slouches back over. With the room lit up, it gives even more disgusting detail on what they see on his back. More flies start swarming around in a frenzy.

"Milk treated me like I was a rabid animal. One day he came down here and told me he'd forgotten to bring me some fresh meat. He said he would take care of it though. He hit that damn remote control and all I could do was sit still. He injected something in my neck and back, the next thing I know it felt like he was drawing some sort of picture on me. Then I felt him slowly tugging away.

"He put me back against the wall and placed a large piece of skin from my back on my lap. He just turned around and walked away. He told me to enjoy myself." His voice starts to buckle for the first time. "Every day, the flies feast on my back. They keep the sores open. They will never heal. Please officer, put me out of my misery."

"I'm sorry, sir, I just can't do th---"

Mr. Gainsborough quickly breaks the glass jar partially filled with water and picks up a large shard. Brooke turns away.

"You seem like a good man officer. I know I did some wrong, but that was a long time ago. I didn't deserve this. Please save Abigail."

Before the detective can react, Mr. Gainsborough fillets his throat and collapses over. Brooke battles the tears falling from her face.

"Detective, please, there can be no more deaths. We have to find a way to Bartholomew. But I don't think it's as simple as just going past that wall for some reason. I think he..."

The wall behind them slams shut.

"What the Hell?" Said the detective and he spins around with his gun and flashlight pointed towards the entrance.

He quickly pulls Brooke behind him and before they can make another move.

"I can't brea... I can't breathe." Brooke collapses.

Chapter 44

Helpless

"There's a time to cry, and a time to rejoice." said Bartholomew. "There's a time to be forthcoming, and a time to yield. There is a time for refreshment, and there is a time for labor. And now it's time to get back to work... Wake up."

Brooke and the detective groggily raise their heads to look at Bartholomew. They have both been restrained in a heavy steel oversized chairs. Brooke can't help but remember the terror in Mr. Gainsborough's eyes, and that Bartholomew was responsible for his demise.

"Now it's going to take you both a moment or two to get your bearings. I'd like to use this time to lay some ground rules. This is more so for you, detective. I feel like Brooke and I are like old chaps.

"I do the talking and you do the listening. I think that's a rather simple concept really. If I need anything from you, which I won't, I will make it known. You are both sitting here against your will and probably feeling a bit helpless. But I give you my word that no harm will come to either of you. Once we are done here, you walk away. Oh, and don't worry about your guy outside. He is sleeping peacefully in his squad car. You can explain everything to him back at the station.

"And I know I said both of you would yield no harm, but I have to tell you I was ready to slice your fucking throat, detective. How dare you interfere in my personal family business. He..."

"Listen you sick asshole, what you are doing is about to..."

"Silence detective!" said Bartholomew in an ear-piercing scream. "You break my rules one more goddamn time and I'm going to rip out your damn tongue and make you watch Brooke eat it. I am not the fucking game... you are!

"Oh my, listen to my voice." Bartholomew quickly downshifts his ire with a look of deep regret on his face. "Detective, you should be absolutely ashamed of yourself for making me use my gutter voice. Brooke, please accept my apologies for spewing such filth from my mouth. You are a lady and certainly didn't deserve that. Besides, I wouldn't dare make you eat his tongue. But I also won't tell you what I really would have done with it.

"Enough of this tired conversation. I only have about 15 minutes, then I need to get out of here. You have seen and heard many things on this trip to the house. One of them still brings me great pain, Thaddeus.

"I loved my brother dearly. He taught me how to read. He stood up for me when no one else would. If he hadn't, my parents would have probably beat me to death. He stepped in and aided me with my research. I made a mistake that cost my brother his mind. And being the type of person Thaddeus was, he always made sure I was taken care of.

"Surely you've heard the term *I'd gladly take a bullet for you.* That term is never one that should be taken lightly. It means that the person that made the statement places so much love and respect into who you are, they'd rather lose their life than to see something as brilliant as yours end.

"My brother took more than a bullet for me, he took a lethal injection and died for me. That's right, Thaddeus didn't kill any of those people. You killed the wrong man. He wouldn't harm a fly. During his last two months here at this house before his arrest, his mental behavior was in and out. He had some good days where he knew exactly who I was and how he got there, but those occurrences only lasted briefly, before he slipped back into this lethargic and humbled role.

"But he was much healthier and healed than he led on. I suppose he figured if he turned himself in pretending to be me, I would stop what I was doing. And while I admire his staunch support and strong conviction, my research just had to be finished. We are entering the last phase. This little television show is almost at the series finale. I'm sure there are still many questions. I promise to give them to you, Brooke. Now, I have another press conference to get ready for in about an hour. I'm thinking I will smash my previous ratings record. OK Brooke, time to go." he said as he walks towards Brooke's chair.

"What do you mean!? What a minute Bartholomew." said Brooke in desperation. "You said you weren't going to harm us. Where are you trying to take me?"

"Look Bartholomew. *Please don't do this.*" said the detective in a begging tone. "You want a hostage, you can take me. Please just let her go."

"I suppose you don't really understand any of this. Brooke will be standing at the end of this. I would never harm her. She has some important work to do. She will never be a hostage. She is my guest. Now, Brooke, if you play nice, the detective can be released from his personal prison in about an hour. Don't worry, detective, this will all be over in a couple of days. I will send you our coordinates for the big soiree soon."

He uses a small device to release the locks on Brooke's chair. "There you go Brooke. We must hurry, mama is waiting for us."

Chapter 45

Behind the Glass

Bartholomew leads Brooke out of the house and to his waiting car parked just behind both squad cars. Brooke is tense not knowing what's next, yet she also has a strange sense of calm, because she believes she won't be harmed.

"This way, Brooke. We are nearing the promise. This story will have its conclusion."

"Where are you taking me, Bartholomew?"

"To a place I'm sure you'll be quite familiar with."

As Brooke and Bartholomew depart, she looks back at the house hoping the detective is doing fine, and that he can leave in safety as promised.

The drive is not long before they reach their destination, in half hour or less. The Cadillac pulls into a garage that closes behind them. As he opens Brooke's door, she pans around and looks at the long metal beams occupying the ceiling. She realizes it's a warehouse, as she can hear workers and forklifts in the distance.

"This way, Brooke. I will give you a grand tour later. I must get mama prepared for her debut. I'm going to have you wait in here for me. I shall return in an hour. There is a television, tablet, and mini fridge. Please make yourself at home."

"Wait a minute, Bartholomew. Whatever you're thinking of doing with your mother, please don't. I know she and your dad scarred you both mentally and physically, but this won't change any of that. Please let her go. She is of no significance to you now."

"You are right, Brooke. She has no bearing on anything in my life right now. I have the power to change and the power to believe. I can make the right decisions, and I can do them right now. How did that sound? Her life means absolutely nothing to me, and I'm about to give her what she always desired, fame. Oh, and one quick mentionable. Every time I hear the name Bartholomew, it makes me think of my dear brother. From here on out just call me by my birth name. It's only appropriate. Now if you'll excuse me!"

"WAIT!" shouted Brooke, but he quickly leaves and locks the door behind him.

She hears another door open, which sounds like its right next to her. Milk cuts on the light, which illuminates a two-way mirror in Brooke's room.

"Hello, mama, how are you doing? Did you enjoy your breakfast? Mama!? Why aren't you speaking? Is something wrong?"

What is he doing?

Brooke can only see the back of Abigail's head as she is sitting on a loveseat in front of Milk.

"Come on, mama, where are your manners? I have someone here I want you to say hello to."

He grabs his mother by her hands and helps her up. He slowly turns her around to the two-way glass.

"Say hello to Brooke, mama. I believe you two have already become acquainted. Don't be shy Brooke, you can wave. We both can see you."

She slowly raises and gestures with her hands for him to stop what he's thinking about doing to his mother. She focuses on Abigail's face. Her eyes are full of terror, yet her mouth is wide open as saliva slowly trickles from her bottom lip to her blouse.

"Don't worry Brooke, mama has not been harmed in any way, at least not yet. I gave her a nice concoction of various muscle relaxers in her face. It's funny how this medicine works when injected in the face. Your eyes and mouth stay wide open for hours. There is nothing you can do to control your muscles until it wears off. I have a few more things that mama needs for our little press conference. These cocktails are my best work. I don't believe there is anything out there quite like them."

He sits his mother back onto the loveseat and removes three syringes from his jacket pocket. He injects them one by one into her neck, right arm, and mid-spine. Brooke can only watch in horror as he smiles at his mother as though she were a sculpted masterpiece.

Chapter 46

Showtime

"OK mama we have 5 minutes till show time. Let's get you over to the studio. Brooke, you can watch us live on your television. See you soon."

He walks his mother out the door, as Brooke watches helplessly.

Wait a minute! The tablet. I wonder if I can get a connection with the tablet.

As she powers it on, she quickly sees that she needs a password to access the internet. Before she can investigate further, the television comes on, which startles her. An announcer voice speaks

"We now interrupt your regularly scheduled programming for an important message."

"Good evening to you all. I apologize for this interruption once again, but I wanted to make sure you all were well informed, and most importantly, entertained."

The camera quickly moves to Milk. He is dressed in an all-black tuxedo complete with tails and a top hat. He wears a white mask over his face. The mask has wording scribbled all over it in magic marker. They look to be words that his mother and father made him repeat often when he was a young boy.

"During my last telecast, I introduced you to four fine individuals. I will provide you with an update on their *progress* if you will. But today I bring to you a treat. I want to introduce you to someone very special. She has been a longtime fan of television and cinema. Today marks her debut on the silver screen. Her name is Abigail Gainsborough. Now before I bring her out, I will give you fancy journalists and law enforcement professions a few moments to search your databases and draw some early conclusions.

"Tick tock… Tick tock! OK, I think that's enough time. Ladies and gentlemen, I'd like to introduce, Abigail!"

The screen quickly moves to Abigail sitting in a chair atop a makeshift stage. She has two black patches covering her eyes. Her mouth is still agape with saliva more pronounced than before. The camera zooms in to her face. You can also see there are ear plugs placed into both her ears.

"Ladies and gentlemen, Abigail is so excited that her mouth is stuck wide open. But that's just fine, because I'm going to speak for her. In fact, I'm going to speak for all of you.

"I'd like to touch on two of three very important dynamics: Choice and self-diversity. We will leave desire for another time.

"Many of the things we believe are based on things that were aptly written where we mercifully yield to another's ideology on any particular said topic.

"Sometimes, our beliefs are stemmed from tradition, which dictates certain values or premises laid down. Advice from a family member, a friend, or a passing stranger can sometimes contain a property within it, that once again causes us to posture or to conform to what becomes for some of us, inevitability.

"Perhaps the process for understanding ourselves and each other is to look at one very distinct yet common option in our lives, Choice.

"There is no other more descriptive or demonstrative characteristic that has the power to mold our essence and existence such as choice. However, choice itself is also an enigma or conundrum much like time, because in order to have choices, you have to make choices.

"Choice is also the precursor of the chemical actions in our brain that allow us to deduce and conciliate the direction of our thoughts. Many of us have the ability to choose: Whom to associate with? Whom to love? Which profession? Which faith? All just to name a few...

"Though, if we chose to associate with the wrong people, it could have an immeasurable negative impact on our lives, decisions, and abilities.

"If we chose the *Right* person to love, was there a better choice? If we choose the wrong profession, it may undermine other opportunities from ever evolving to fruition. This can have a direct impact on our families and the very way we live.

"There are countless faiths. Is there ultimately only one God to choose from? To understand choice and the answers to the aforementioned questions, we need to understand another important dynamic... Self-diversity! Are *we* really important? What allows us to be tantalizing, intriguing, demure, and at times ubiquitous?

"Our character defies conventional wisdom because it, along with logic only exists in a tertiary world we've created in our heads to offer superficial benefits.

"How we think, the way we feel, and the way we convey these emotions are based on inert nepotism that is ingrained in us before we have the chance to properly grasp and breathe.

"We are merely slaves to our own thoughts, which ironically are by-products of someone else's illusionary self-instruction.

While choice allows us to believe, self-diversity allows us to colonize this behavior into a vehicle that chases the elusiveness of hope.

"I'm sure I've lost most of you long ago, but that's OK. The train is coming folks, and there is nothing you can do to stop it. You either hop aboard or you let the wheels grind your meaningless bodies beneath it.

"Enough of that, our gracious guest has agreed to assist me with some groundbreaking medicinal breakthroughs. Abigail has been injected with three different blends of serums that I created. They have some amazing effects on the body. Once injected with 5 cc in each syringe, her body entered a heightened sense of awareness in less than 30 seconds.

"Her five senses: Hearing, taste, touch, smell, and sight have increased about 5000%. What does that mean? Well, allow me to show you.

I'm going to remove one of the patches from her eyes. I'm going to shine a dying and dimly lit small flashlight into her eye. Mind you I'm about eight feet away."

He taps the flashlight a few times in his hand and shines it into Abigail's exposed eye as the camera gives an eerily close perspective. Her pupil swells to 1.5 times its size before turning completely white. The saliva runs more rampantly out of her mouth.

"Do you know what just happened? Her eye thought it had been compromised by a light so bright, that the muscles in it bursts. She is now completely and permanently blinded in that one eye. Isn't it amazing how this works?" He slowly removes the patch from the other eye.

"For my next demonstration, I'm going to remove one of the earplugs from her ears in case you didn't notice she had them in the first place.

He lowers his voice to a whisper, and walks inside a small booth, which completely muffles any sound.

"Now, just like her eyes, her ears are extremely sensitive. Right now, my voice probably sounds like the loudest most deafening concerts she has ever attended, even though I'm in a soundproof booth. Trust me when I tell you she could hear a piece of lint drop to the ground with precision. Say Abigail, have you ever been to a concert? By the wide-open mouth expression, I'm assuming that means yes folks. No doubt a heavy metal fan."

He removes a quarter from his pocket.

"Heads or tails? What do you think Abigail?"

He gently steps outside the booth and flicks the quarter forward in the air, letting it hit the wooden stage supporting Abigail. Blood slowly flows from her right ear.

"Another great performance folks. This time, from the sound of quarter hitting the ground, her ear drum was completely obliterated.

"And now for the grand finale. Our gracious guest Abigail will be able to put all five of her senses together. I introduce you to *Capella*. It's really simple engineering, yet breathtaking to look at. It's a small fan that opens up into beautiful metal Peacock feathers. The ends of the feathers are sharpened reinforced titanium. It sits upon a small pole pedestal that is integrated into the floor. I'm going to move out of the way, so Capella and Abigail can have some one-on-one time."

He moves to the side, as he removes the remaining earplug. Abigail still sits, unable to move, but certainly able to see what lies before her. Milk presses a button on the wall and the Capella opens into a frightening display of slowly rotating blades. From atop the blades, you can see the illusion of Peacock feathers. The device starts its progression.

"As the blades get closer, she will lose the hearing in her last ear. As it gets closer, she can see all the engineering that went into making this masterpiece. She can also smell the blood dripping from her right ear, and the stench of salvia continually falling from her mouth. As the blades get closer, they will revolve slowly, yet precisely. They will cut away at her throat as she gets to use her final two senses… taste and touch.

"The pain she feels is incomprehensible, but certainly well deserved. You can now join the stooges." he said.

The blades penetrate her throat slowly and methodically. Milk carefully reaches over and lifts up her head by her hair as the blades completely cleave her head away from her body. Milk releases her head as it rolls down to the ground.

"I have zero remorse for what just happened. If you thought this was beautiful and creative, wait until you see what I've planned for our other four friends.

"Some of you probably wonder why I do this. What is the purpose? Maybe you even wonder how many have already needlessly suffered. So on and so forth, and I don't care. I don't give a damn one bit.

"I don't kill because I'm sick. I kill because you are, and I have the solution."

Chapter 47

Engineering Bliss

Seconds later, the camera switches to the terrified faces of the four victims. Only their heads are initially shown.

"Here are your four friends," said Milk as he changes the orientation of the camera to focus on them individually.

"This is number one, Maria Delphine. As you will recall her shape is a square. She is number one because she was the first person I chose to assist me with some wonderful research. Her shape is a square because of this wonderful device."

As the camera zooms away from her face, you can see her body is affixed to the wall by a device that has her legs and arms spread out. The tears run down her face looking for their escape.

"This device is hooked into over 2000 pieces of her skin. Once I power it on, it will slowly stretch her flesh apart in four different angles; up, down, left, and right. In about an hour there will be constant tension. In twelve hours, the blood will be flowing rather nicely. In twenty-four hours, her flesh will be completed cleaved from her body.

"Number two on the list is Darla Forte. Her shape is round. Pay special attention to the sphere."

As the camera pans back, Darla's head is the only thing that extends from a large metal ball.

"You can't see the inside of this fantastic device, but her body is able to move freely inside. There's lots of room in there, though I suppose that won't last. You see the inside of that circle is going to continually get smaller and smaller. She will have to find creative ways to contort her body. At the twelve-hour mark, both of her legs will be broken in ways that are irreparable. In twenty-four hours, her body will be crushed into a ball about the size of her head.

"I now turn our attention to number three, Mr. Curtis Lanker. His shape is rectangular. I really like this device too."

As the camera pans back, Curtis is lying inside of a rectangular metal box. There are two large metal poles, one each at his hands and feet. Both arms and feet are cuffed and mounted to a thick chain affixed to each pole.

"I'm sure at some point in your lives you've heard the term *drawn and quartered*. Well, this is a derivative of that. As the poles rotate, the chains will become tighter. In twelve hours, there will be so much pressure on his spine that it feels ready to separate. But that's where this machine truly shines. The cuffs will loosen and automatically readjust. At the twenty-four-hour mark, his arms and legs will be slowly and excruciatingly plucked from his body at the exact same time his spine is snapped in two from the pressure.

"And last but certainly not least my good friend, number four, Brendon Skiles. His shape is my favorite, Triangular."

The camera pans back to show Brendon sitting on a small bench inside a glass see-through triangular room.

"This one is my most simplistic, yet my favorite by a long shot for some reason. What you behold is a small room just big enough for one person to sit in. You'll notice the top or point of the room is fluted. In that large vat right above his head, I filled it with a grand selection of moist human feces. I'm going to pump that through the fluted part of my beautiful triangular hourglass. At the twelve-hour mark, he better be standing, because the waste will be near chin level. Each hour after that, it will go past his mouth level and into his nose, unless he swallows a certain amount of it. At some point, he'll only be able to eat so much.

"So, there you have it. Engineering at its very best. You better hope Brooke can figure this out. Game over in twenty-four hours."

The camera quickly show's Milk's hand with a remote inside of it. He presses a button, and the sounds of machines in the background can be heard.

"Time is running out!"

Chapter 48

State of Panic

"Yes governor I understand," said Chief Jared. "I will give them all the information we have. I will call you back in half an hour." The chief looks disheveled.

"Detective, I am extremely grateful that you made it out of there alive. This shit has hit the fan in ways this department has never experienced. The president called the governor. He wanted to make sure we were on top of this. He has allocated some additional resources should we need it, which basically means we better use them. She has to give him hourly updates. The whole nation is now looking at us. This is the most important case that this department and even our entire goddamn state has ever seen. Our asses are on the line with this one. We have to get Brooke back and we have to save those people."

The chief's phone rings.

"Chief Jared speaking."

"Chief, we got another one of those wackos claiming he's the guy in those videos." said the officer. "But somethings different about this one. Do you still want to take these calls sir?"

"Yes, I do. Go ahead and patch him through."

The chief places the phone on speaker so Detective Engler can hear the conversation.

"This is Chief Jared. How can I help you?"

"Well, hello, Chief Jared. I must admit that I'm impressed with the speed of getting through to you. I wonder how many calls similar to this you've gotten."

"Over forty to be exact." said the chief. "You are number forty-one."

Detective Engler motions quickly that the caller is Bartholomew Gainsborough. They turn on the tracing equipment.

"How do I know I'm talking to the real person behind the videos?"

"Well, that's quite simple. Ask the detective if he enjoyed the conversation with the man chained to the wall. I'm sure his smell was inspiration enough. And as I promised him, he was able to leave the house with no problems, although he may have had a bit of a challenge waking up the other officer. But more importantly, tell him that Brooke is safe and sound. In fact, she's watching television in another room right now."

"OK, I'm convinced Mr. Gainsborough. What do we need to do in order to bring Brooke and the rest of those people to safety? I don't want to see anyone hurt. What is it that you are seeking?"

"If it's all the same to you, please call me, Milk. Please rest assured that no harm will become of Brooke. But you must also understand that the other four will have to experience pain. How much and to what degree will be entirely dependent upon you.

"I will leave you a clue. This clue if solved, will bring you directly to me, Brooke, and the other four. Your clue is this… A better way, a better product, a better you.

"Once you solve that easy puzzle you will be well on your way. And since I'm such a cool guy, I'm going to give you some advice. Bring lots of heavy digging, drilling, and cutting equipment. Oh, and don't worry, I haven't rigged the place with explosives or anything else cliché like that. You'll just have to figure out how to get in. You better hurry up, I'm sure our friends are starting to feel some discomfort." He disconnects the call.

"Did we get the trace?" asked the chief.

"No sir, no sir we didn't. Dammit!"

"Alright detective, this is the 4th quarter with no time remaining and no timeouts. We are on the goal line, with one more play to go. We can make no mistakes. Find out what that phrase means and ready our units. We're about to put an end to this once and for all."

Chapter 49

Spilled Milk

It's been an hour since Brooke witnessed the most heinous thing she had ever experienced. She looks around frantically for a way out, but to no avail. She flips back on the television reluctantly, knowing the whole country is once again abuzz. Surely enough, it's all over the news and on every channel.

My phone must be going bat-crazy right now. I hope mom and dad are OK. Something tells me they're on their way here. I must find a way to help those people. This is insane.

The sound of a key unlocking the door flutters her heart.

"Hello Brooke, by the look on your face, I can tell you are bitterly disappointed in me. But don't worry, I just got off the phone with Chief Jared. I gave him some information that will allow his department to help everyone. I imagine they will be here within an hour or so. Come... I have prepared something for us."

As Brooke follows behind Milk, she wishes she had something that could subdue him. But she also wonders even if she had such a thing, would she even use it?

"You have shared with me things that I'm sure you've never discussed with anyone else," said Brooke. "These people that you placed in those devices are not your voice. This is not who you are. I am here with you right now. You don't need those people anymore. Please let them go."

"You speak the truth. I don't care anything about those people anymore. Whatever happens to them at this point makes very little difference in this grand scheme of things. There is nothing that defines me. I have never had a voice, Brooke. But now I will. The world will know of me. They will study me in a frenzy, I will become an underground cult hero. I will have books written about me. Hell, I may even have a movie made based on my life story.

"But that's not my contribution. I will leave behind things that will make man better. There's no need for the rat in the maze mindset to continue. I will change history as we know it.

"Now enough of that for now. I had Chef Kunira from Bravo's prepare what I believe to be your favorite dishes. We have rosemary and ginger lamb chops, Mediterranean couscous, fresh grilled asparagus, and made from scratch key lime pie. I had him prepare me everything but the key lime pie. Because of some of the ingredients used in it, I would become terribly sick. How's that for irony? Your mother names you Milk and you're also lactose intolerant. And please don't say you aren't hungry, because I know you are. This will be the first and last time that we officially dine together. And no, that day at the café certainly doesn't count. Please have a seat and join me. Does everything look wonderful to you?"

Brooke internally breathes a huge sigh. She knows that this is all part of his design. She needs to continue to play by his rules if she is going to have any chance of saving those people.

"I have to admit that everything looks amazing. Thank you for putting this together. How did you know these were my favorites?"

"Your question and the answer will make sense very soon. For now, let's eat."

There is an uncomfortable yet expected silence, as Brooke musters up the courage to ask Milk questions that are still mysterious to her. But her mind is also on the four victims. So much time has passed since the live telecast. She knows they are in great pain by now.

"When did the killing start? Why did you start doing such a thing?"

"I knew we would discuss this at some point. I wondered when your journalistic baton would start twirling again. Well, the first time it happened, Thaddeus and I bought some horses to liven up our property. One day while we were outside enjoying the day and walking around the property, this guy comes to our gate and flags us down.

"I believe he was a drifter, but he seemed to be a really nice guy. He told my brother and me that he had been riding for many years and was even able to tell us a bit of history about the horses we had. He asked if he could take one of them for a ride around the property. We both thought what the heck, and let him in.

"He saddled up and mounted like a pro. He took our horse, Argentina, for a few laps around the property. It was difficult for us to hear him, but it appeared he was yelling at our horse. When he brought the horse back, he jumped off and said we had the worse horse he had ever ridden. He smacked Argentina across her beautiful mouth, like she was some type of cheap whore.

"Something snapped inside of me. I had a chain and heavy padlock in my hands from the other stable's entrance. Without hesitation I swung the heavy lock hitting that bastard right in his nose. He fell to the ground screaming as blood gushed like a geyser. I recoiled the lock and kept hitting him and hitting him, until I had smashed in his skull.

"Thaddeus was confused at first, but he seemed to understand it was necessary. The feeling that ran through my body was amazing. I felt this huge sense of relief. The rush was unlike anything I had experienced before. It was then and only then that I admired my parents. If they had the same feeling in beating and humiliating me as I did in bashing that man's head in, then I could do nothing but respect it."

"So, is it still fair to say that you attribute your parents as being the catalyst to opening this door?"

"Well, I don't have any chemical imbalances, Brooke. I suppose if my parents were normal and treated me like they treated my brother, things may have been different. If my parents were loving like yours, maybe I could look in the mirror with merriment instead of dismay. They were the worst of the worst and they both died like the pigs they always were. I have zero regrets about my course of action for either of them. Well, that's not true. I wish I had done it sooner."

"What about the other's? The original eight victims, including the governor's niece. What did they do to you to deserve such a horrific death?"

"It had everything to do with my mentor Dr. Roland Saflin. I have already explained how important his research was in introducing nanotechnology into medicine. When he first unveiled his research to his colleagues, it was hailed as a landmark in medical breakthroughs. He was lauded as a hero, though that would prove to be short lived.

"When word leaked out about his research to the general public, they quickly rejected his ideas as another person trying to play God at the expense of human lives. They wouldn't give him the opportunity to discuss or even debate why his work was so revolutionary.

"There was a huge lobby organized by seven people. They rallied up enough local support through scare tactics to force an early vote on funding for his project. It was defeated by a narrow yet resounding vote. It was shortly thereafter that the Dr. had a stroke and was forced to retire. If he had the funding to continue the research, his vision would still have been realized. Instead, it was relegated to an idealism of another quack doctor."

"What a minute!" said Brooke. "This sounds exactly like a story I reported on several years ago, but it was a different doctor. This doesn't make any sense. It was one of my first important assignments."

"No Brooke, you are correct. It is the same story. For most of his profession, Dr. Saflin was known as Dr. Golden Weeks."

Brooke instantly recognizes the name.

"He was given that name by a colleague when he did a very risky heart procedure for a patient. The patient was terminal and had been seen by five other doctors. He had been in the hospital for over six months and prior to meeting Dr. Saflin, had no ambitions on ever leaving there.

"The good doctor performed an extremely high-risk surgery. In fact, so high risk that it was only attempted one other time. Guess who did it the first time? That's right, my mentor.

"The patient had a miraculous recovery and was able to leave the hospital on his own accord without assistance in three weeks. Those three weeks would go on to be called the *Golden Weeks*. And there goes your history behind the name. Let's take a walk, I want to show you something. I appreciate you dining with me, Brooke. This means a lot."

Milk leads Brooke to another room. When he opens the door, her knees buckle.

"What is this!?" she said, as she twirls around the small room slowly. The walls are all plastered with news articles and pictures of Brooke. As she walks closer to inspect, she sees her whole career in front of her showcased like a sick prize.

"You were the only one that supported the good doctor, Brooke. You made a plea in your reporting for us as a society to embrace these types of rare miracles in medicine. You probably thought this was an insignificant story that would just go into your journalistic archives, kinda like that tomato festival you covered as one of your grunge jobs.

"But no, your reporting did not fall on deaf ears. In fact, your appeal resonated with Dr. Saflin. I learned about you some years ago from him. I've been following your work ever since. But for me, there were also other reasons attached. I promise to explain them to you shortly.

"You wanted to know about the original eight people. Well, the first seven people were evil. They were cowards! They needed to pay for what they did to the good doctor's name. The eighth person was the governor's bitchy niece Valerie. One late night as I was returning home from a trip, there was some ruckus on the intersection. I pulled over at a safe distance to watch. I saw three teenage boys beating and stomping on what I found out to be a homeless man. This girl jumps out of the car, squats over the homeless man, and urinates all over him. She told the man that he shouldn't bother to tell because her aunt was the governor, and that she would have his ass thrown in jail for good if he even tried.

"They were all so drunk, but there was no excuse for what they did. I pulled over to the man after they left and tried to help him up, but he had already died. They beat him to death. I decided to take vengeance for the poor sap.

"The first seven were quite easy to lure. I simply invited them all to a benefits dinner at my estate. They didn't know it had belonged to the good doctor. They just knew they were getting some free food, and possible monetary resources for their rogue group. And you already know about the end result of that meeting.

"Valerie was fun to lure. For such a smart girl, some of her decisions were incredibly dumb. I posed as the chair of the National Governor's Association. I told her it was a complete surprise, but this year we were nominating her aunt with an achievement award, which would be presented by all of her peers from the other states. I asked her if she would like to be a part of the festivities by doing the introductory speech. Of course, she was excited to be a part of it. I made her swear not to mention any of this to no one, not even her mother. She met me at one of the local hotels, and I took care of things from there.

"Our time together is running out, Brooke. It seems like the lead I gave your police friends paid off. They are just outside the perimeter of the warehouse trying to find a way in. Please open the chest on the far wall. It's something I've been saving for you."

Brooke walks towards the chest being ever deliberate in her moves. She wonders what the end means for her. As she opens the chest, there is a white gown inside with a costume tiara.

"I've been saving that for many years. You were meant to have it, Brooke. This is what you are. Please put it on. When you are finished, open the door on the other end. I'll be waiting for you."

As Milk exits, she stands there looking at the dress. It is a ball gown that looks in like new condition. But the smell of the gown gives its age away. Faintly, but distinctly, she can hear the sound of drilling.

The chief and the detective are here. I have to do this. I have to save those people. God, please watch over me and help us all end this nightmare.

Brooke puts on the dress and tiara. She hadn't noticed it before, but there is a small mirror just to the left of the exit door. She glimpses at herself before she exits. She changes the look of perplexity and fear on her face to one of ease. The end was near.

Chapter 50

The Angel of Death

Brooke exits the door and steps into a room whose beauty and complexity cannot be denied.

"Brooke--you look perfect. You look just like an angel." said Milk as he presses a button on the wall.

"This is my favorite room in this place. It's the only room that's built to sit just over the lake behind this warehouse. I thought this would be fitting to further accentuate your beauty.

"Every plant and flower in this place were flown in from locations all over the world. The lighting and temperature must be just right. There is such a delicate balance of life in here. You must treat each of them with love and affection in order for them to grow and thrive. If you don't, they will all die. The job of a parent should follow that delicate order. Sadly, too many of us never get to share that experience.

"Mama tried to share a moment of beauty with me one time. As I was sleeping one night, she came up to the attic and asked me if I wanted to see something beautiful. I was excited of course, because she wasn't like her normal self. I could tell she wasn't going to punish me.

"She had something behind her back, but I couldn't see what it was. She told me to turn and close my eyes until she was ready. I complied while eagerly waiting. She told me to turn around and open my eyes. I was in shock. I had never seen mama look like that.

"She looked just like the angels I had always heard about. Her face was all made up, and she had on the prettiest dress that I had ever seen. She wore a tiara on her head. She twirled around and asked me if I thought she was beautiful. I told her she was the most beautiful woman in the world. I was so excited that I was about to clap, but she quickly told me to keep it down, so not to wake anyone.

"She walked over to me and told me she was an angel. She grabbed my hand and placed it under her gown. I didn't understand what was happening. I was so confused. She kept my hand there and made me maneuver it while she made strange noises. She removed my hand and told me she would kill me if I ever said anything. She turned around and pulled the dress and tiara off and left them sitting on my floor. She put on her robe and went back downstairs. I must have washed my hands for an eternity that night.

"I despised her for what she did, but I could never forget the image in my head. She was the most beautiful woman I had ever seen. I folded up the dress and kept it with the tiara in my drawer. When I ran away that night, I took it with me.

"A couple of years ago, you attended a formal Black and White Gala. You wore an absolutely gorgeous dress. As soon as I saw it, I had that flashback. I wanted to experience that feeling one more time. And now you proudly wear it, looking even more beautiful and stunning. You are pure and without any audacity of perversion.

"I look at you as the perfect example of what humanity should be, Brooke. Your convictions are strong, and you are not marred by the temptations that test the integrity of most. You defended my hero, making you one in the same. It also makes you the most beautiful woman I have ever seen. But there is also another exceptionally important reason why you are here. Something that Dr. Saflin was not aware of.

"But before I go off into those details, I realize I haven't given you much as it relates to where all of this research was going in the first place. Dr. Saflin, through his engineering wizardry, created computers the size of a grain of rice. These computers worked in tandem with one master mainframe. That mainframe was the brain.

"The doctor's sister was injured in an automobile accident and lost the use of her legs. Before she died from other complications surrounding the accident, he promised her that he would find a way to help the paralyzed walk again.

"And that's where his research took off with those Nano-computers. The good doctor was so close. In the end, the stroke and his paranoia got the best of him. The solution was right there in front of his eyes, but he was completed blinded by it.

"Perhaps he was also blinded voluntarily, because he knew I was born to continue his research. Ingrid Sellers was my first demonstration of engineering perfection. Prior to your meeting with her, I injected her with a serum that turned off certain Neuro-transmitters in her brain. She basically forgot how to walk. That was nothing but pure science you experienced that day as she waltzed down the embankment.

"I am hoping you now understand that the good doctor and I weren't playing puppet master, we actually had some legitimate work that yielded phenomenal results."

"But Milk, you and the doctor killed all of those people. So many innocent lives that were lost. So many of them tortured. Regardless of the end results, the methods you used to obtain them are reprehensible. Those people didn't…!"

"Please accept my apologies for rudely cutting you off, but we simply don't have the time to debate. We did what was necessary. The sacrifice of a few will yield a new era for many.

"Now, there was another critical piece of research the good doctor was working on. This research was on the medicinal side of the equation. Research that will prove to be unsurpassed.

"I'm sure you are already aware of one extremely rare and unique trait that you possess. You are one of 12 people in this word with the Rh-null blood type. So rare that only 43 people have ever been recorded with this blood type. There is no time for a history lesson I'm afraid, but I want to show you how special your blood type is. Please come this way."

Milk walks Brooke over to a lab table filled with beakers of various unknown fluids and a high-powered microscope.

"Brooke, may I see your right index finger? I want to administer a small prick to draw blood onto the glass. If my calculations are correct, I will be able to show you something truly miraculous."

Brooke complies, seeing no harm in only a spec of blood being given. Milk takes her sample and mixes it with three additional samples from a droplet. He placed the combinations back under the microscope.

"It worked!" said Milk. "I can't believe it. The doctor was so close. I did it, Brooke. This is an amazing day. The most amazing in human history. Please take a look for yourself."

Brooke looks through the microscope.

"What is it that I'm looking at!?"

"Watch as you see the red cells merge with the yellow ones. Prior to today, those cells just bounced off one another. Now, the red cells not only merge, but completely destroy every remnant of the yellow cells. What you have before you is the cure for Aids, leukemia, cancer, heart disease, and the list goes on and on.

"The doctor was on to something in his research, but he was missing some key components. The most important was the Rh-null blood type to act as the perfect binder. Do you know how significant this moment is?"

Before Brooke can answer, there is a loud thud sound at the door.

"The cavalry is here for you, Brooke. There isn't much time. Here take this. These are my final notes on the research I was doing. This will provide the medical community with the know how to be continually lazy. I've done all the work."

He removes the glass from beneath the microscope and places it into a black padded bag filled with similar looking fluids.

"All of the people I used as test subjects were all lower than dogs. They deserve no pity, and I should have killed them all once I was done with my research.

"Oh, and take this." he said as he reaches into his pocket removing a flash drive. "You can give this to the chief. It will show him how I was able to cripple the state's system and have my way with it. I'm sure this technology may come in handy.

"All I ever wanted to do was to grow up and experience life with everything it had to throw at me. I have this opportunity now, but it was only meant to be short-lived. I have no future, but I have plenty to leave behind.

"I will have the dual pleasure of being known as a serial killer and a savior. I know that you will give my story the respect that it deserves. And now your final task. I hope I have given you enough information for a satisfactory story. I wish I could be here to see all the hoopla over you. It's certainly well deserved."

"Wait a minute. What do you plan to do?" asked Brooke, as there are now loud drilling noises in the background. "Whatever it is you're thinking about doing, it's not too late. Now, you and I both know that you won't be roaming the streets anytime soon, or perhaps even ever. But you have such a unique opportunity to teach. Your ideas and research will advance medicine in ways never before discovered. What if you could continue to be a part of that?"

"It is a grand idea, Brooke, and one with merit. But I am quite tired you see, and I miss my brother dearly. I made a promise to him that once I finished the research, I would join him on a trip around the world. I'm going to keep my promise. It's time for me to join him."

He pulls from the wall a long and narrow covered drawer, reminiscent of how bodies were filed in old mausoleums.

"Brooke, sitting here next to me are three coolers filled with ice. I would like to donate my organs to research. This fine machine will allow me to do so. This is my last invention. I call it the extractor. As I lay down in it, there are robotic arms attached inside running on a program that will extract my brain, heart, liver, kidneys, and eyes. All the good chief has to do is make sure they go into those coolers. I did all the work. And because I'm such a curious creature, I'm doing this without any anesthesia. By the way, I also shared my engineering expertise on that flash drive. Again, do with it what you will.

"Goodbye Brooke, you're still green under the collar, but you're going to make a fine journalist. One of the very best."

"Milk--WAIT!"

The door bursts off the hinges as the swat team quickly fills the area with lasers pointed at Milk. He quickly enters the box and seals it. The Swat Team surrounds Brooke as they can only hear the sounds of sawing and screaming coming from the box. Brooke clutches the flash drive and closes her eyes. *It's finally over!*

H. Eugene

Epilogue

60 Minutes interview, one month later

B rooke, what you have just told us on this news channel, and on behalf of those that are watching or listening, allow me to say thank you." said Mr. Ephram

"You have taken us on a ride through the mind of one of the most dangerous serial killers this world has ever known. And for someone so depraved and vile, he has given us hope and a new beginning for all. You are now a household name around the country. What do you plan to do with this newfound fame?"

"Thank you for such kind words. I am very fortunate to be here to tell another side of the story. I will never forget the things I witnessed, nor the things I've been told. What I will do is embrace today. I want to do all I can to make a significant impact on the things I can affect. What that translates to, is I will be right back to work on Monday, doing what I love."

"And there you have it. Brooke, thank you again for joining us."

On the flight back home, Brooke has the opportunity to unwind and think about her future. This story was the toughest of her young journalistic career. But this is just the type of story that she needed. Her next one will completely stretch her mind.

H. Eugene

Acknowledgements

I would like to thank some individuals that helped to make this book a reality for me.

Tracee – What can I say? Team HT… you are a fantastic mentor and a wonderful artist. My writing continues to blossom because of you.

Jill – Best WW ever! Thank you for being such a huge part of this project. Your opinions and guidance have been critical to my growth.

K.D. – A personal and heartfelt thank you my friend. Your influence on my writing has been impactful and meaningful. Thank you for your support and your guidance. We have much work ahead of us.

To Steve, Raydale, Bessie, Sharon, and Tracee … Thank you for your awesome help on making the book trailer.

Thank you, Braylen, for your inspiration in helping me with some critical ideas.

Sandra – I would not dare write another book without giving you a special public shout out for all your support.

www.ingramcontent.com/pod-product-compliance
Lightning Source LLC
Chambersburg PA
CBHW051944220626
47052CB00004B/787